PUFFIN BOOKS

What Will the Robin Do Then?

Jean Little is the author of more than twenty books for children, including *Mama's Going to Buy You a Mockingbird*, *Mine for Keeps*, *Different Dragons* and *His Banner over Me*. She has won many awards for her work around the world, and her books have been translated into braille, French, German, Dutch, Danish, Norwegian, Greek and Japanese. Jean Little lives on an old farmstead near Elora, Ontario.

What Will the Robin Do Then?

Winter Tales

JEAN LITTLE

*The north wind doth blow
And we shall have snow
And what will the robin do then, poor thing?
He'll sit in the barn
And keep himself warm
And hide his head under his wing, poor thing.*

—Mother Goose Rhyme

Puffin Books

PUFFIN BOOKS
Published by the Penguin Group
Penguin Books Canada Ltd, 10 Alcorn Avenue, Toronto, Ontario, Canada M4V 3B2
Penguin Books Ltd, 27 Wrights Lane, London w8 5TZ, England
Penguin Putnam Inc., 375 Hudson Street, New York, New York 10014, U.S.A.
Penguin Books Australia Ltd, Ringwood, Victoria, Australia
Penguin Books (NZ) Ltd, CNR Rosedale and Airborne Roads, Albany,
Auckland 1310, New Zealand

Penguin Books Ltd, Registered Offices: Harmondsworth, Middlesex, England

First published in Viking by Penguin Books Canada Limited, 1998
Published in Puffin Books, 2000
1 3 5 7 9 10 8 6 4 2

Copyright © Jean Little, 1998

Publisher's note: This book is a work of fiction. All names, characters, places and incidents either are the product of the author's imagination or are used fictitiously, and any resemblance to actual persons living or dead, events, or locales is entirely coincidental.

Manufactured in Canada

CANADIAN CATALOGUING IN PUBLICATION DATA

Little, Jean, 1932–
What will the robin do then?

ISBN 0-14-130152-X

1. Children's stories, Canadian (English).*   2. Children's poetry,
Canadian (English).*   I. Title.

PS8523.I77W46 2000   jC813'.54   C99-930821-1
PZ7.L7225wh 2000

Visit Penguin Canada's website at **www.penguin.ca**

for Pat

*my sister, my friend
and my shelter whenever
"the north wind doth blow."*

Contents

Three of the poems in this collection have been previously published in my book *When the Pie Was Opened*. "Goodbye, Tizzy" first appeared in an anthology called *Window of Dreams*. "Without Beth" came out in a collection of ghost stories, *The Unseen*. Both stories have been revised for this book.

Preface

One summer afternoon, twenty years ago, I began reading my novel *Look through My Window* aloud to my nephew and niece. Nine-year-old Sarah was fascinated when I started telling them why I had written the book.

"When your mother was eight and I was fourteen," I said, "our father bought this marvellous old house . . ."

Mark, who was eleven, interrupted me at that point.

"Aunt Jean, don't tell us all that stuff," he begged. "I want to believe in the story."

I knew exactly how he felt. I, too, wanted to believe in the story. So I told Sarah "all that stuff" when Mark was out of earshot. Yet later I realized that it is possible to do both. I, the writer of the story, always know how it began and what parts of it are based on actual events and places. Yet, at the very same time, I am caught up in the plot and the characters are as real and alive to me as Mark and Sarah. So those of you who don't want to know, skip to the stories themselves. And those of you who, like Sarah, are curious about the seeds from which these particular stories sprouted, keep reading.

Although I now read prefaces as a matter of course, I never read them when I was a child. I could not imagine wasting time reading the author's preamble to her writing when I could read the writing itself instead. I wondered why people wrote such things as prefaces. I know now. Either they cannot resist explaining themselves or their editor suggests the exercise. In my case, my editor gets the credit. But I plan to enjoy doing it.

Prefaces seek to answer the question why: why was this particular book written or why did it take this shape? Although I chiefly write longer fiction, I have also written many poems and short stories. I write one whenever I am seized by an idea which, to my mind, does not call for expansion into a novel. Sometimes it springs from a small incident in my own life, sometimes from a question which I need to answer, occasionally from somebody else requesting or, perhaps, challenging me to write something. Usually, although not always, the core of the story takes place within one or two days. I step into the lives of my characters, live with them while they work something out or see something differently, and then I step back out, leaving them to go on with their lives. Author Katherine Paterson told me once she believes that in a good story, "Something has to happen and somebody has to change." I think that in my short stories I often seek to explore what prompts change and capture the moment when change takes place. I don't do this consciously and it is not equally true of every story in this collection. But one of the chief things I loved about *The Secret Garden*, when I read and reread it during my childhood, was watching Mary grow.

I wrote the stories over many years and badly wanted to have them published. Realizing I could group several together under a winter theme, I worked to turn them into a manuscript I could submit to my publisher. I know winter is technically only three months long but in Canada the first hints of it appear long before December and last long after, so the collection includes stories from September to March. I had to revise some of them, shifting them to new seasons, to make them fit my scheme. Then, as punctuation, I "framed" each story with two poems. I haven't the patience and stamina necessary to try to publish single poems and yet I hate to see them piling up, unread, in a drawer. Choosing them was pure joy.

The title story had two beginnings. One took place years ago when I was teaching a class of disabled children. As the first snowflakes floated down, I asked my students if any of them knew a song about winter. One small boy, who lived a hard life and never fussed about it, astonished me by beginning to sing, "The north wind doth blow . . ."

"Who taught you that?" I asked, astonished that a child who seemed so impoverished would know this old song.

"My mother," he said proudly. "She's English, you know."

Years later, my mother happened to be present when a family of "boat people" were given a carton of used clothing. They had a five-year-old boy and, in the box, was a fancy pink coat with a white fur collar intended for a girl. The little boy tried it on and revolved so his family could see his magnificence. Mother managed to make them understand that he should not appear in the coat on his first day in a Canadian school. It was not easy because they knew little English but she managed. She came home outraged at the donor who had not troubled to check the sex of the Vietnamese child. I have known several kids like Edward who have too many loads to carry and yet keep marching on, bearing others' burdens. I admire their resilience, their dogged optimism and their courage.

"Goodbye, Tizzy" came from my wondering about the child who raised my first Seeing Eye dog, Zephyr, until he was old enough to start his dog guide training. Zeph was, like Tizzy, an exuberant yellow Lab. The Seeing Eye did not give students any information about who had raised the dogs. The child who brought Zeph up must have loved him the way Dinah loves Tizzy. Writing the story was my way of saying "thank you."

"The Hallowe'en Masquerade" had its genesis when my three-year-old great-niece Jeanie went out on Hallowe'en for the first time. She looked as cute as a button in a clown costume my sister bought for her but she was clearly a little ambivalent, especially when she was told, "Nobody will know who you are." At three, you have barely grasped your separate identity and you do not want to risk losing that precious self. Since we live in the country, we had to drive her from house to house. In the car, on our way home, her small voice said shakily, "I don't want to be a clown any more. I just want to be a person."

The story "Without Beth" also sprang from a real incident. I had written a play for our church in which one of the characters was my Aunt Gretta, who had been a missionary in Taiwan for many years. She had died before the play was written. My mother, her sister, agreed to play the part and even wore Aunt Gretta's clothes and used her cane. Just before the performance, she looked out into the audience and was shaken when she thought she saw Aunt Gretta sitting there. Someone spoke to Mother, distracting her momentarily. When she turned to look again, the seat where she had seen her sister was empty. She did not tell me about this until several hours later. Mother was not someone who saw ghosts but she found the experience both unsettling and comforting. When Janet Lunn asked me if I could write a "ghost story," I remembered Mother's experience and wrote "Without Beth."

I once spent the last two or three hours of Christmas Day with a boy who had passed his time, from early morning until late afternoon, being hustled from one house to another. At each place, he opened gifts. He was never allowed to settle down to play with them, however. Instead he had to leave them behind and be driven off to yet another relative's home. He was the only child in our family gathering that Christmas and I felt great sympathy for him. He was so angry and frustrated and had no outlet for all that bottled-up fury. As he finally settled down and told me in detail of his favourite presents, I resolved that someday I would write about his predicament and, in my story, the kid would rebel, go on strike, break free from adults' expectations and grab hold of his Christmas.

"A Mantle of Praise" was inspired by the verse of scripture quoted in the story.

"Charlotte's Celebration" was written for all those kids who, like Charlotte, have no real family celebrations in which to play a part.

"Freddy Frisbee Finds a Home" started when I first heard of "smart houses." These domiciles could be programmed to take care of all your needs. Freddy arrived from his orphanage in answer to such an unhomelike idea.

"City Boys" was written after an urban family with two sons built a house next door to ours and started farming. My city boys are not the real ones but I am grateful to them for starting my imagination working. I myself have been a "city girl" for most of my life. It used to puzzle me why people who were not farmers would choose to live outside cities. They were so far from the library, for one thing. Five years ago, my

sister Pat and I bought an old stone farmhouse standing on ten acres of land and moved in. Now I cannot
bear the thought of having to return to a setting
where the moon has to compete with streetlights,
where you cannot sing as you walk to the mailbox and
where you lack the blessings of space and quiet. The
wolfhound and the hedgehog in the story are real and
share the farmhouse with us.

Jonah, in "The Night of the Next Straw," is
fictional but the house he lives in and the tombstone
in the Auld Kirkyard in Fergus are really there. I, like
his mother, am often tempted to walk out the door in
the middle of a family fracas.

I was invited to write a story about a library for an
upcoming anthology. "Somebody's Girl" was the result.
I am glad that the people who commissioned it settled
for a different tale since I soon knew that I wanted to
include Rose's story in my own book. Who is Rose? She
is myself after my mother died, perhaps, but mostly she
is herself. I loved the old book *Nobody's Girl* when I was
a child and, after I grew up, I bought a secondhand
copy which I let Rose's grandmother own.

A friend, reading through this collection, asked
me if I had intended to write stories about children in
"dysfunctional families" and another pointed out that
most of the characters are facing loss. I did not choose
the stories for that reason but I am moved by how
children manage to survive despite drastic change and
loss. I do not think of families as "dysfunctional"

either. I live in such a family and, despite our differences from run-of-the-mill, cosy, regular families, we continue to funtion day after adventurous day.

I was also asked why I put so many twins in so many of the stories. The reasons are not the same for each set. Sometimes I simply want to have more children who are around the same age and so share in the same activities. Occasionally, twins emphasize the aloneness of their single sibling. Sometimes, when the main characters are twins, I want two children who are closer than most brothers or sisters. "Without Beth" would not have been nearly so credible if the girls had not been identical twins and Nick and Holly, in "The Portable Christmas," had to both be born on Christmas day. I doubted their mother could have hit that date with two unconnected births.

The poems speak for themselves, I believe. I wrote the first draft of "Rain" when I was in high school. I wrote "My Mother Got Me" last month. I loved choosing which ones to include.

I hope you enjoy the collection because I have other stories and poems which are clamouring to get published. It will only happen with the enthusiastic support of my readers.

Jean Little
Elora, Ontario
June 1998

What Will the Robin Do Then?

September

Apples

Kindergarten was over and done.
Jessica Fay was in Grade One.

Her teacher's name was Mrs. Prout.
On the second Wednesday, she gave out

Reading Readiness Workbooks. She
Told the children to do page three.

"Apples are round. Apples are red,"
Living Language Workbook said.

And APPLE was printed, nice and big,
Under a circle attached to a twig.

Though Fay was only six, she knew
That what the book said was not true.

But she didn't put up her hand and tell.
She coloured the round, red apple well.

She didn't go over the lines one bit.
When her page was done, she was proud of it.

Still, even back then, Fay knew enough to be glad
    that apples are really apple-shaped,
    bumpy, tall, crooked, squat,
    hand-sized, pocket-stretching,
        Streaked with green and splashed with yellow,
        astonishing,
        friendly
    and wonderful . . .
Like language.

Goodbye, Tizzy

Dinah Archer wakened with a yelp as a cold, wet nose poked against the sole of her bare foot.

"So help me, Tizzy," she bellowed, rearing up on one elbow and pulling her feet back to safety, "if you do that once more . . ."

Her words broke off abruptly. Tizzy would not get even one more chance to shock her awake that way. Tomorrow morning Tizzy would be gone.

All Dinah wanted to do then was bury her face in the pillow and cry. She blinked hard to keep the tears back. She was the one member of her family who never cried. Tizzy already thought she was taking too long. Tizzy wanted her breakfast.

Dinah swung her feet out of bed and leaned forward to give the big dog a loving swat. But the Labrador retriever was no longer there. She had wheeled about and gone galloping over to the door. Dinah grinned and stayed put. Tizzy, realizing her mistress was not moving, came flying back to encourage her.

"Okay, okay, you big idiot," the girl said. "Wait till I put my shoes on. You can hold out that long."

Dinah didn't take time to dress. She'd throw a jacket on over her pajamas when she got downstairs. Tizz was still only a year old and when she said she needed to go out, she meant it.

Tizzy watched as the girl put on the first shoe. Then, as she bent to reach for its mate, the dog decided to help. She dove after it and their heads collided with a crack.

Dinah gasped and swayed. She felt as though she had been struck by a sledgehammer. Tizzy seemed not to have felt a thing. She gave the sneaker a playful shake and thrust it onto her mistress's lap. Her tail kept wagging the whole time.

"Ouch!" Dinah said. She blinked, waited for the spinning to stop and then went on sternly, "If you want me to hurry, dog, don't knock me out first. Your head is like a boulder."

Tizzy's look said Dinah was fussing over nothing. She turned her rock-hard head and stared fixedly at the door. The girl gave in. As she got to her feet, Tizzy whirled about in a mad scramble of paws and dashed across the room once more.

By the time Dinah reached the hall, the big dog was already hurtling down the stairs ahead of her. Her tail was whamming against the wall. Having been whipped by that tail often, the girl knew how hard it hit. Boy, Tizzy was tough.

As they reached the kitchen, Tizzy bounded ahead, cavorted around in a joyous circle and made as if to

6

jump up on the girl. Dinah took a quick backward step and spoke sharply.

"No, Tizzy. Phooey!"

The yellow Lab instantly landed back on all four feet and looked apologetic. The look said she would never have jumped up, not really! She was sorry, though, that she had given her mistress the wrong impression.

Dinah laughed in spite of herself.

"You clown," she said lovingly and went to get her dog some breakfast. As she lowered the dish to the floor, Tizzy's nose plunged into it. By the time Dinah had set the stainless steel bowl down, a third of the food was gone.

"Whoever gets you won't have to worry about her dog guide being a picky eater," the girl said. Her voice was husky but the Lab was too busy bolting her food to catch the change in tone.

At last, facing the fact that every crumb was gone, she sighed, burped and turned on Dinah a pleading gaze that said she was still starving. Every other morning of the ten months she had had the dog, Dinah had hardened her heart. But today was different. She shot a glance over her shoulder to see if Mum or one of the twins was coming down the hall. They weren't. Dinah snatched up the bowl, added another generous scoop of dog chow and offered it to Tizz.

Gulp, crunch, gobble! Tizzy disposed of the evidence in a flash.

Dinah grinned, crossed the kitchen, grabbed her windbreaker and took her dog outside. As the Lab ran off across the yard, the girl stood still, taking in the beauty of the morning. Although September was only half over, Dinah could see her breath misting in the frosty air. There would be more warm days but winter was hovering, ready to pounce on them.

Not yet, Jack Frost, Dinah thought, and she shivered in her thin jacket.

Tizzy looked back to see why her girl was just standing there.

"Park time," Dinah called. "Hurry up. It's cold out here."

The sun had broken through the clouds. Now the entire sky was blue and the wind against Dinah's face felt warmer. She should have been pleased but she scowled instead. It ought to rain on the day she was losing Tizz.

If it had poured though, she would have had to stay inside, enduring her family's pitying glances. As it was, she and Tizzy could take the tennis balls to the pasture later and play.

A noise from inside the house told her the rest of her family was stirring. She winced as she thought of facing her twin sisters. They would be so kind! Each of them had raised a pup for The Seeing Eye three years ago, and they thought they knew all about what she was going through. They were wrong though. They didn't understand. How could they? Buster and Sasha had been okay but Tizzy was special.

8

As she thought this, Dinah heard further activity in the kitchen. Mum had been down earlier, of course, to have breakfast with Dad. Now she was back making sure the twins didn't skip their orange juice and die of scurvy. You'd think they were six instead of sixteen. They were so spoiled.

Tizzy was checking out the bushes. Dinah hugged herself and went on listening to the sounds from inside, water running, dishes clinking, and a radio voice giving a newscast. Then one of the twins spoke in a high, carrying voice.

"Where's Dinah? Isn't this the day they're picking up Tizzy?"

"She's outside," Mum said, a note of warning in her quick answer. "Yes, this is the day. But keep your voices down."

"The poor kid," the other twin chimed in, lowering her voice half a decibel. "It's awful when they come. I was heartbroken when I had to give up Buster."

The twins' voices were alike but Dinah knew that had to be Karen. She was the one who wanted to be an actress. Hearing her actressy voice dripping with sympathy made Dinah feel like throwing up. Thank goodness Kathy had more sense. She only planned to become a scientist and win the Nobel Prize.

"I'm going to be a vet," Dinah told Tizzy, who was not attending. "Or maybe a teacher."

"It was hard for you two," Mum was saying now, "but I think it will be far harder for Dinah. You had each other and lots of school friends to help you through it. Dinah just has Tizzy. She'll be lost without that pup. It worries me."

"If only she weren't so serious about everything," Kathy said with a sigh. "And so shy around other kids. I keep telling her to relax . . ."

"She's like your father. Reserved. She's also in your shadow. She had to act differently or she'd be swallowed up . . . Oh, I can't explain. But it hasn't been easy for her having twin sisters."

"I'll bet she's crying her heart out. Maybe I should go out and try to cheer her up," Karen said.

"No, Karen. Don't," Mum began.

It didn't work. Dinah was horrified to hear Karen's chair scraping back from the table. She did not wait. She fled. Without a backward glance, she raced across the yard, through the belt of trees and down the side of a field until she reached the long stretch of pasture. Tizzy bounded along at her side in huge, joyous leaps. Dinah knew the dog was delighted with this surprising turn of events. Catching Tizzy's mood and filling her lungs with the crisp autumn air, Dinah, too, suddenly felt a spurt of wild joy.

So what if she only had on a jacket over pajamas? So what if her runners were already soaked with dew? Even freezing to death would be better than having to be comforted by Karen. One thing was sure, Dinah was staying out of reach until she was positive the twins had gone. Luckily, she herself didn't have to go to school. Mum was letting her stay home.

By the time she would next have to face her sisters, Ms. Foster, from The Seeing Eye, would have come and gone. After that, she would be so miserable that nothing they said or did would matter.

Tizzy was not worried. She was cavorting around Dinah in enormous circles. Usually they did not come to the pasture until after school or until the Saturday chores were done. Dinah eased the tennis balls out of her windbreaker pockets, trying not to rip the seams again.

"Go get it, Tizz!" she yelled, hurling one ball the length of the field.

The dog, flying after it, was a cream-coloured blur. Her golden brown ears streamed back in the wind. She looked so beautiful skimming over the rough ground that Dinah's throat ached.

"Way to go," she called, doing her best to sound excited. "Bring it, girl."

Tizzy did not need to be told. She was a retriever through and through. She dropped the ball right at Dinah's feet and waited eagerly for the other one. She was so unsuspecting. She had no way of guessing that this game would be their last.

Dinah kept playing automatically as she thought about Tizz being taken from her. She had already considered lying, telling Ms. Foster that the dog had started biting people or running away. If she was not suitable as a dog guide, Tizzy would be offered to the Archers as a pet.

But Dinah could not lie about her. First of all, Mum

would know better. Second, Tizzy was so perfect that nobody would ever believe she was mean or incorrigible. So that was out.

The thing Dinah could not bear was picturing her dog at The Seeing Eye waiting for her mistress, her own girl, to come and get her. She would wait and wait and Dinah would not come. When that happened, would Tizz imagine Dinah had stopped loving her?

No. She knows I love her. But she'll stand by the door and watch . . .

"There goes the bus. Let's go in," Dinah called. "It's my turn to eat."

Mum kept Dinah busy all morning tidying her room. After lunch, she said the three of them should go in to Morristown. She had to get groceries and return some library books.

"It'll keep your mind off things," she said.

It was easiest to go along.

"I'll do my other errands first," her mother told her, pulling up in front of the library. "I'll meet you here in an hour. You go on in and look at books or give Tizz an extra walk until I come."

Dinah was standing watching the car drive off and trying to decide what to do next when she saw the blind man and his dog guide coming toward her. Tizzy strained on her leash, wanting to rush over and make friends, but Dinah held on with both hands, keeping her dog's bouncy enthusiasm in check.

"Phooey, Tizz," she muttered. "Quit that."

The man reached the curb and the golden retriever stopped and waited for a command to go forward.

"Good girl, Bella," her master said, as warmly as though she had just pulled him out from under a speeding bus.

As Dinah thought this and heard him say, "Bella, forward," an enormous truck, going far too fast, came barrelling at them. Where it had come from Dinah had no idea. She gasped. But, when it disappeared in a cloud of gritty dust, Bella was still standing on the opposite sidewalk. She had ignored her master's command.

"Wow," Dinah breathed. The golden retriever had saved his life by disobeying him. "Intelligent disobedience," Ms. Foster called it.

Dinah was so impressed by their narrow escape that she relaxed her grip on Tizzy's leash. At once, Tizz, who was only a year old and unused to city traffic, lunged forward and dashed toward the dog on the opposite curb.

"Tizzy, PHOOEY! COME! NO!" Dinah shrieked, losing her cool completely. She ran out to reclaim her dog, sure that if she just stood where she was, Tizz would grow confused and double back and be run down before her very eyes.

Brakes squealed. Another truck had come out of the blue. The driver swerved but still hit Dinah a glancing blow. She was sent spinning and landed at the blind man's feet. When she stopped sliding, she was flat on her face with her forehead resting on his shoe.

Tizzy's nose poked her anxiously.

"Don't, Tizz. Good girl," Dinah croaked, forcing herself to sit up and grasp Tizz's choke collar in an unsteady hand. "I'm sorry, mister. I . . . Oh, Tizz, quit! I'm ALL RIGHT!"

"Bella, sit," the man said. "Rest. Child, are you really all right? What happened exactly? Is this dog yours?"

"I guess I'm okay," Dinah said slowly, feeling scrapes on the heels of both hands and a bruise on her right knee starting to throb. The truck, which had come so close to knocking her down, killing her even, had slowed for a moment and then sped away.

"He's gone," she said. "It was a truck. The driver didn't run over me, just knocked me down."

She got up stiffly, glad the man could not see how red her face was. She had been a prize dope and she wanted to cry again. But the man was being so nice and Tizzy would be upset if she burst into tears.

"This dog must be yours, I think," the blind man said as Tizzy left Dinah to nose Bella's ear.

"Oh, Tizz, stop that," Dinah wailed. "Your dog's wonderful. Mine is bugging her and she is just sitting there like a statue."

"Bella is an extremely intelligent and highly educated dog," the man said, smiling and stooping to stroke the dog's head lightly.

"Tizzy's going to be a dog guide too but I don't think she'll ever be that good. I can't even get to the library without an accident!" Dinah told him, her voice shaking.

"Let's go into the library and sit down for a few minutes," the man said. "I'm Alan Kent, by the way. Bella and I are going to the library anyway. How's Tizzy in libraries? And what's your name?"

"Dinah. Dinah Archer. The library's one of the places I bring her to get used to people," Dinah told him, limping across the street at his side.

Tizzy, taking a leaf from Bella's book, trotted along as though she already had graduated. She was sure Dinah's fall had been her fault and she was keeping a low profile.

Mr. Kent was really nice. Dinah had never talked with a blind person before, not without anyone else being there. You saw them training on the streets of Morristown every day and Ms. Foster had brought a blind lady and her dog guide to Dinah's 4H group to talk about raising pups. She had been young and funny and even really pretty but she had not spoken right to Dinah. Mr. Kent, though, was easy to talk to, like Dad.

They entered the library in friendly silence.

"You find us a place to sit down," Mr. Kent said. "Bella will follow. You need to catch your breath and I want to tell you how grateful I feel to you for raising a dog like Tizzy."

Dinah went to a reading table with chairs around it. She found she was glad to sit down. Her knees had begun to tremble.

"Why are you grateful?" she asked, as he settled Bella down beside his chair.

"I never had a chance to thank the family who raised Bella for that first year but I've always wished I could."

"Oh," Dinah said.

"How long have you had Tizzy? And is she the first dog guide you've raised?" Mr. Kent asked quietly.

Dinah opened her mouth to answer and felt a great lump closing off her throat. She managed to choke out, "I've had her for a year. They're coming to get her at three o'clock today."

Her voice broke and she could not say another word.

"What a day to get knocked down by a truck!" Mr. Kent said. "Now you've caught your breath, are you sure you aren't hurt?"

"I'm sure."

"Good," Mr. Kent said gently, busily scratching first Bella's velvet ears and then Tizzy's.

"What will happen to Tizzy?" Dinah burst out. "I mean . . . what will happen to her tonight? Will the blind person be there waiting?"

It had all been explained but that had been months ago. She could not be sure what she had been told.

"I'll tell you all I know and about my meeting Bella," the man said. "Before my class started, she'd been tested to be sure she was physically fit to be a dog guide. Veterinarians examined her. Her hips were

X-rayed to be sure she wasn't getting hip dysplasia. Quite a few tests. They didn't want her to have over-sensitive pads on her feet or to be traffic-shy. When she'd gone through that, and I know they were very kind to her, they gave her to her trainer. Instructor, maybe I should say. She worked with her for four months, teaching her all the things dog guides must know. Bella absolutely adored that instructor. I was definitely second fiddle to her for a while."

"How do you know?" Dinah asked, her bruises and scrapes forgotten.

"Well, for one thing, when the instructor left Bella and me alone together, my dog went to the door of the room and cried. I said, 'Bella, I'm your new master.' But she went right on crying."

"That's what will happen with Tizzy. I know she'll miss me. She hates me to leave her," Dinah said.

"Of course she does. But, Dinah, even though Bella got excited every time she saw her instructor go by, she was making friends with me. If a dog has been loved the way you've loved Tizz, she has lots of love to give others. Bella didn't pine away and Tizz won't either."

Unable to speak, Dinah waited for more.

"I had a dog guide before Bella and, when he retired, he went to live with my brother. I was sure Perky wouldn't settle but he soon followed my brother everywhere and he loved him until he died last year. Tizzy will be fine. I can tell you've done a great job."

Tizzy had her head on Mr. Kent's knee, lapping up

the attention. Bella glanced up now and then like a grown-up watching a little child.

"Dinah!"

It was Mum. She came over and Mr. Kent stood up and was introduced.

"You have a great daughter, Mrs. Archer," he said. "And she has a great dog there. Dinah had a tumble earlier and I suspect she's got some bruises to show for it. Perhaps she needs a dog guide to keep her safe!"

"I can see she's added yet another rip to her jeans," Mum said, but she sounded sympathetic. "We'd better go, Dinah. We have an appointment..."

She stopped there and Dinah managed to say good-bye. On the way home, she told her mother all about her encounter with the man and Bella's saving Mr. Kent from stepping out in front of the truck.

But as they turned into their lane, her eager words dried up. The Seeing Eye van was in front of the house.

Ms. Foster had come for Tizzy.

Mum parked the car, got out and went to meet the woman.

"I'm sorry we weren't here when you arrived," she said. "It's a lovely day, isn't it? Perhaps winter won't come at all this year."

Dinah sat where she was, hearing her mother's voice being polite and Ms. Foster's being polite back but not moving to join them. She felt frozen. She was not ready. It couldn't be now. She needed more time.

Mum opened the back door of the car and Tizzy, all

18

unsuspecting, scrambled out in an awkward dive. The Seeing Eye representative stooped to pet her.

"Hi, Tizz, you beautiful girl," she said. "Yes, yes. You adore me. Hi, Dinah. Come on out. I want to hear if Tizzy is still being as wonderful as she was last time we talked."

Dinah got out of the car. She bobbed her head at Ms. Foster and let her mother go on filling in the silence. Her lips felt stiff and, if she said one word, she was going to bawl like a baby. She mustn't. It would be cruel to cry and have Tizzy taken away worrying over her. Somehow she had to be her usual self. Already her dog was looking up at her with puzzled eyes.

Then Dinah felt Ms. Foster's hand patting her shoulder.

"Well, I can see for myself that she's in great shape," she said. "How about if I take her right away? Saying goodbye is tough. Dragging it out makes it tougher."

Dinah still could not speak. Tears had begun spilling down her face, in spite of all she could do. She went down on her knees and put her arms around the dog's neck. Tizzy licked Dinah's cheeks, nose and right ear. She snorted into the girl's neck and it tickled.

Dinah gave a croaky little laugh and rose. She nodded at Ms. Foster.

"Want to go for a ride, Tizz?" Ms. Foster invited and slid open the side door of the van.

Tizzy loved going places. She leaped in joyfully. She did not look around for Dinah until Ms. Foster closed the door. Then she peered out the window, her expression only slightly anxious.

Ms. Foster went to the rear of the van and reached in for something. When she had it safely in her arms, she carried it over and set it gently down right at Dinah's feet. It was a wriggling black bundle with outsized feet, round astonished eyes and a comical air. A black Lab puppy. It cocked its head on one side just the way Tizzy often did. Then it stood up, sniffed Dinah's ankle and began playing tug-of-war with her shoelace. As Dinah moved her shoe away, the pup gave a funny little growl and chased after it, pouncing on it and holding it down as though it were fighting back.

"Good boy," Dinah said automatically, through her tears. The pup wagged its whip of a tail furiously.

"He's looking for a home for the next year," Ms. Foster said, smiling at the puppy's attempt to drag the lace out of Dinah's sneaker. "Your parents say it's up to you, Dinah. His name is Button. He won't take Tizzy's place, of course. No other dog will ever do that. But he does need somebody to love him and you are good at loving. You've done such a great job with Tizzy. She'll be a superb dog guide."

"Phooey, Button," Dinah said before she could stop herself.

Then she leaned down, detached him from her shoe and lifted him up into her arms. He was warm and silky-soft and eager to cover her face, neck and ears with puppy kisses. She knew at once why he had been named Button. His nose looked exactly like one. Now he was busy licking at the spot on her shirt where she had spilled a blob of ketchup.

Dinah laughed.

Then, over the top of the puppy's head, she caught sight of Tizzy still watching her. Instantly she thrust the pup into her mother's arms and ran to the van.

"I love you best, Tizzy," she told her dog through the glass that separated them. "Be like Bella. Be even better!"

She wanted to say goodbye but her voice cracked and no more words would come.

Tizzy was beginning to be worried. Her tail stopped wagging. Dinah had mopped away the first flood of tears. She didn't want Tizzy's last memory of her to be of her crying. More tears kept brimming up in her eyes but she fought to keep them back. She could see through them and she could smile. It wasn't a good smile but Tizzy's tail began to move again ever so slightly.

"Shall I leave Button?" Ms. Foster asked.

Dinah nodded but her eyes stayed fixed on the beloved face framed by the van window. Ms. Foster got in and turned the key in the ignition.

Still Dinah stood steadfastly gazing at her dog. She went on standing there, watching and waving, even though Tizz was soon lost to sight in the bright blur of tears. Dinah did not turn until she could no longer hear the van. Then she knew Tizzy had really gone.

Button yelped shrilly. Mum had put him down and gone in to answer the phone.

"Somebody, pick me up this instant," the yip commanded.

Slowly, Dinah reached down and gathered him up. Holding him cradled against her chest, she put her lips close to his ear.

"I'm glad you're a boy," she whispered. "Good boy, Button."

Button understood. He yawned and leaned against her. He stopped squirming and trying to get down. He put his head into the hollow of her neck and fell asleep.

"What a surprise for Karen and Kathy," her mother called. She held the door open for girl and dog to come into the house. "Your dad and I decided not to say anything to them in case you didn't want to raise another one."

"He's asleep," Dinah said as though her mother could not see. "I'll take him up to my room. We can nap together."

Her mother almost said, "Don't let him up on the bed. Remember that dog guides aren't allowed on beds."

Then she let the words go unsaid. Tomorrow would be soon enough.

Me and My Shadow

Whether she likes it or not,
My shadow has to follow after me all day.
. . . Except sometimes she slides around corners
    Before I'm quite there
Or ducks into hidden alleys
    to wait for me.

Who cares? I am still the boss.
When I sit down, she has to sit down too.
When I stand up . . .
Well, it is true that my shadow often
    lies down on the job.
Although I am in a rush, she likes taking her time.
She leans on houses and props herself against
    every passing tree.

She won't stand up for herself.
I'd say she was afraid of her own shadow—
    if she had one.
Even when I just take two or three menacing steps
She's off like a streak of dark.

She is soft-hearted, my shadow.
She never hurts anyone or anything.
When she stretches out on the grass,
She doesn't break a single green blade
    or flatten one scarlet maple leaf.
She lets the goldenrod grow through her.
When a spider longlegs it across her face,
    she doesn't slap it away.

Not that she has a face exactly.

She has no substance to her, no weight.
"You're unreal," I tell her.
"Before you get too proud," she murmurs,
"Try jumping on me with both feet."

Once in a while, I've caught her
    talking behind my back.
She says the strangest things.
"She's not as tough as she looks,"
I've heard her whisper.
"She's afraid of making a fool of herself.
Right now, she's lonely. She feels like crying.
Don't let her fool you.
She needs you.
That toughness you see is all an act."

"Who are you talking about?" I ask.
She doesn't answer.
I look down on my shadow, so flat, so dependent.
But what if she sees through me?
Those whispers make me nervous.

"Why do you insist on tagging after me?" I snap
     at her.
"What good are you?"
"As long as you can see me," she says gently,
"You will know that you are walking in the light."

"And when the light goes," I challenge,
"Where will you be then?"

"I am a part of the dark," says my shadow.
"I will come with you.
I will give you the stars."

ctober

Rain

Rain is as bent on mischief as a child.
She pokes the Thunder's ribs until he roars.
She perches on proud roofs and thrums her heels
And tickles grass and taps on solemn doors.

She drenches garden parties, flattens curls,
Paints saucy freckle faces on the roads,
Makes mud and then, good-naturedly, gets down
To scrub the tiny, blissful backs of toads.

Hallowe'en Masquerade

When Mick realized that Hallowe'en was on one of his father's weekends, he told himself he couldn't care less. Before his parents' divorce, Dad had either been away or uninterested in most of the smaller holidays.

"Hallowe'en is just an excuse for greed," he had said more than once. "I wasn't allowed to go out and collect quantities of candy from strangers when I was a boy."

He had sounded proud of this fact but Mick, knowing that his father had grown up on a remote farm in northern Manitoba, thought his dad might have gone out if there had been anybody living nearby. He didn't ask. He had heard more than he wanted to about his father's stern boyhood.

Dad was scornful about Valentine's and St. Patrick's Day too. He had even made fun of the Tooth Fairy until the day Jessie, age six, had lost a tooth and burst into tears because she was convinced the Tooth Fairy would not come near their place since Dad had insulted her.

Celebrating any holiday, big or little, was planned for and carried out by Mick's mother, who acted as though she couldn't hear her husband's belittling remarks. All three kids soon learned not to discuss costumes or party plans in front of Dad. Celebrating was Mum's department.

Mick was grateful to his mother for all the years of neat Hallowe'en get-ups but this year he was nearly thirteen and Hallowe'en was no longer a big deal. You had to be younger to go out asking for "trick or treat" or older to be going to a party. He was caught in the between time.

"I can ask him to change his weekend, if you like," Mum said to him and his sisters. "He wouldn't care."

"No," Jessie protested. "I want Merri to see my costume. She'll love it."

"She should," their mother said, trying not to meet Mick's eye.

Mick had wondered about Jessie's costume. Mum had always helped them come up with clever ideas. Dad was useless and he had often been annoyed over the time Mum spent turning Mick into a robot or an enormous crocodile with working jaws.

"You can buy outfits for Hallowe'en," he had snapped just before he had told them he was leaving. "It's ridiculous to put so much effort into making something homemade when you could be doing something you really enjoyed."

"Or something you really enjoyed," Mum had said,

continuing to stitch sequins onto Jennie's tutu. "I like making costumes."

"Have it your own way," he had said and left the house, banging the door so hard that the pictures on the wall jumped.

The door had banged a lot throughout the last six months he had lived with them. Then he had gone and things had been peaceful for a while. But, before their divorce was final, he had gotten an apartment and Merri, his dental nurse, and her small son Tim had moved in with him.

"Barbie to the life," Mum had muttered.

She had not known Mick had heard her but he had grinned when, this year, she had talked Jessie and Jennie into dressing up as Barbie and Ken. She had even come home with real wigs for them. Jennie's long blonde hair came down below her seat. Mick wondered if Dad would get it. He doubted it. Dad still thought Merri looked special.

"She reminds me of the angel on the Christmas tree," he had confided to Mick once. "Or the Blue Fairy."

Mick had not replied. He thought Merri was cute for a grown-up but not terribly bright. She couldn't talk with him about any of the several things he was interested in. When he asked if she played chess, she smiled sweetly and said she had never tried but her favourite games were board games like Life or Monopoly.

"What about you, Mick?" Mum had asked about

Hallowe'en. "Have you got a costume in mind?"

"No," he had said, laughing at her. "Forget it. I'm too old. Also I have a project due. Hallowe'en is for little kids."

"I guess you are growing elderly at that," she had said fondly. "Just promise me not to outgrow your Christmas stocking for a few more years."

"It's a promise," he told her.

Dad came for them on Friday right after school. Jessie and Jennie were lugging their costume boxes and yammering away like a couple of blue jays so their big brother was not required to say much.

"No costume, Mick?" Dad asked, putting his gym bag into the trunk of the car.

"No costume," he said and got into the back before his father could suggest he sit with him. He pretended to doze off there and did not answer any remarks that came his way. The long, long weekend of being polite to Merri and the Wimp would begin soon enough.

Merri DID look a lot like Barbie, he thought, as she and her little boy came out on the balcony to wave to them. And the kid was a dead ringer for Christopher Robin.

"Hi, Mick," the little boy called.

Mick snorted and went up the steps in one giant leap that carried him out of sight of his stepmother and stepbrother. Dad made no comment as he opened the door but he did not look pleased. Thank goodness Jessie and Jennie kept up their babble and drowned all awkward moments. Then they were getting out of the elevator and saying hi.

"Hello, Michael," Merri said in her little-bitty voice.

"Hi," he tossed back.

Tiny Tim looked up at him with wide, startled eyes. He must have caught the irritation Mick thought he was keeping undercover. He did not even say "Hi" back.

Then, the minute Mick was starting to arrange his stuff to make his room seem a little less frilly, Merri called them to supper. When he got to the dining area, he saw Merri's parents were also there. He remembered them from the wedding.

They were sort of fluffy, he thought, sweet faces, puffy hair, roundish glasses, Hawaiian clothes. Even though they were different sexes, they looked as though they must be brother and sister. And they smiled the same sunny smile.

"Are you going out on Hallowe'en this year, Timmy?" Grandma asked Mick's stepbrother.

Tim, four years old and shy, gazed at her and spoke not a word. Mick could tell the kid was thinking hard. Sure enough, when he DID speak, he showed what a silly he was.

"What's Hallowe'en?" he asked.

"What's Hallowe'en!" the twins shrieked in unison, staring at him.

"You get dressed up and go out and knock on doors

and ask for candy. Don't you remember?" his granddad said.

"He was sick last year," Mick's father told them. "But he helped Merri hang up a jack-o'-lantern cut-out on the door, didn't you, son?"

Tim was clearly not sure he remembered. But he had seen jack-o'-lanterns on "Sesame Street" so he nodded.

"I got you a clown suit this morning," his mother said. "It's adorable. The hat has the cutest little pompom and the outfit is beautifully baggy. When you have it on, nobody will know you, darling. You'll fool everybody."

Mick watched the little boy's face. He was pretty sure the dopey kid did not like the idea of nobody knowing who he was. Well, wasn't it an alarming idea? If you were four and you'd been kept all cosy and snug by Merri and your nanny, anything out of the ordinary might freak you out.

"I don't want it," Tim said softly.

Nobody but Mick heard him. If they had, Mick knew, they would have laughed and teased him about being silly. He waited for Tim to decline his costume again but Tim stayed silent. Maybe he, like Mick, had known he'd be laughed at.

Merri made the four-year-old try on the clown suit before he went to bed. There was a funny fat red nose with an elastic to keep it in place. The pant legs were baggy and there was a cap with a fluffy pom-pom on top.

"Stand still, baby," Merri told Tim as she put make-up on his face.

Jessie and Jennie would have squirmed but Tim stood like a little doll.

"Go look in the mirror now," his mother laughed. "You are so cute. You'll love yourself."

While Jessie and Jennie cooed over him, Tim stared at the clown in the mirror. His grandparents chuckled delightedly at the picture he made. Dad, who had gone back to his office, telephoned and Merri went to another room to get the call. Mick, who meant to go and work on his school project, found himself stalling.

"Who can that little clown be?" Grandpa teased. "I've never seen him before."

"He's such a sweetheart," said his grandmother with a big smile.

Tim stood absolutely still, not responding in any way. Mick got up and went over to him. Not making a big deal out of it, he took off the clown nose.

"It looks fine," he said. "Don't get your blood in a bubble, kid."

"Thank you, Michael," Tim whispered.

Mick felt he had done more than enough. Leaving them all making plans, he departed for the privacy of his room. He understood, for the first time, why Dad so often went back to work right after supper.

Jennie and Jessie had a Hallowe'en party at Brownies the next afternoon. They were to wear their costumes and they could bring a guest.

"Let's take Timmy," Jennie said. "You'd love it, wouldn't you, Tim?"

"No, thank you," said Tim, sounding extremely positive for once.

"But it's lots of fun," Jessie said. "There'll be a haunted house and you get to feel dead eyes and things. In the dark! You wear your costume and nobody recognizes you."

"I don't have a costume," Tim said.

"Your clown suit's your costume, Timbit," Jessie said.

Tim ran away to his nursery rhyme room with the comforting baby wallpaper.

"I guess he's too little," Jennie said.

"Or too shy," said Jessie.

The year before, Merri had insisted they could not light a candle with a three-year-old around, but this year, Dad brought home a great round pumpkin and Tim helped scoop out the stringy insides filled with seeds. Mick was persuaded to do the actual carving of the face. He gave it long sinister teeth and thin slanting eyes. Tim backed away from it, his own eyes wide.

"It's neat," he quavered in a thread of a voice.

"Give it a kiss," Mick teased.

Tim paled.

"It doesn't like me," he mumbled.

Even his doting mother laughed. Mick was the only one who guessed that Tim might actually believe what he was saying.

After supper, the two girls got dressed up as Barbie and Ken. Merri thought they looked marvellous.

"Your mother is so clever," she said wistfully. "I don't know how she comes up with ideas like that. I just went to a store for Tim's clown suit."

Mick looked at her and then looked away. He felt slightly ashamed of his mother and a tiny bit sorry for poor dumb Merri who would never get the joke.

Then it was time to go out the door. The girls each had a pillow case for their loot and they were all agog with excitement. Tim, however, flatly refused to go with them. Dad had come home to escort them. Yet, no matter how they all coaxed, it made no difference. The little clown backed into a corner and burst into tears.

"Oh, let's go," Dad said, annoyed and impatient. "He's too young anyway."

They left and Merri was busy answering the door.

Mick told himself to keep out of it. Tim was not really his brother, whatever Dad said. But he could not help it. He remembered being frightened by lots of things when he was Tim's age. He went over and sat down next to the small boy. He saw that Tim's whole body was shaking.

"Hey, buddy," he said, his rough voice strangely soft. "Want to come out with me? You could ride on my shoulders and you'd be safe as . . . safe as houses."

Tim's uncertain, wondering gaze took him in.

"Why? Do you like clowns?" he asked.

"Not especially. You're not really a clown though,

38

Tim. It's just pretend. Come on. We could have fun."

Tim stood up. He drew in his breath. Then he moved a tiny distance toward his stepbrother. Mick grew impatient. Stepping forward, he swung the small boy high and placed him squarely on his shoulders.

"He's coming out with me," he told a wide-eyed Merri and, before she could say a word, the two of them were out in the black night.

"Who could this adorable clown be?" said the neighbours. "I can't think. Nobody we know, that's for sure."

"Tim, say 'Trick or treat,'" Mick told him.

"Trick or treat," Tim yelled from his safe perch.

They marched on, passing witches, goblins, space aliens, Power Rangers, black cats, vampires, robots and ghosts. Tim clutched Mick's hair when a skeleton drew near but calmed down when Mick patted his foot.

"What's your name, Bone Man?" Mick asked.

"George," said the skeleton in a growly but very much alive voice.

"I knew it wasn't real all the time," Tim declared.

"I know you did," Mick told him.

Then, long before Mick was ready for it to end, it was time to go home. Tim, set down outside the door, pushed the bell.

Merri opened the door, started to say "Hi" and then, warned by a gesture from Mick, waited for the small clown to speak. He stood in front of her. His big red nose was gone and his make-up was streaked. His clown hat was crooked. But he was not the crybaby he had been an hour before. He had cut at least one of the apron strings which had been keeping him from growing into a boy.

"Trick or treat, lady," he shouted.

Merri jumped. Then she reached into the big bowl of candy and handed him three molasses kisses and a bag of peanuts.

"Who do you think I am?" Tim demanded cockily.

For the first time since he was born, his mother felt unsure what to say to him. At last, catching Mick's eye again, she got her act together.

"I don't know, little clown. Are you Bozo?" she asked tenderly.

All at once, Tim's new confidence wavered. What if she really did not know him? His eyes filled with tears.

"I don't want to be a clown any more," he quavered. "I want to be a person. I want to be Tim."

Merri went down on her knees and hugged him tight.

"Timmy honey, it's just pretend," she said. "You are always my Timmy even when you're a Hallowe'en clown. Poor tired baby, I can see you're ready to be tucked into bed."

Mick waited to see how the little boy would take this. Was he going to turn back into Tiny Timmy after their evening of adventure? Or would he make a push to stay free?

Tim sniffed, wiped his nose with his sleeve and

recovered himself. He wiggled free from the too-tight arms.

"My name is Bozo, the Hallowe'en clown," he shouted, astonishing his mother and making Mick practically burst with pride. "Hallowe'en clowns don't ever go to bed."

"I have a great bedtime story to tell you, Bozo Tim," Mick offered, grinning at the little boy. "It's about a skeleton."

"Not at bedtime, Mick," Merri began.

"Okay, Mick," said Bozo, reaching for his step-brother's hand. "Clowns love spooky bedtime stories. Mum, is there another Hallowe'en next year?"

"Yes," said his mother faintly.

"Well then," said the dirty little clown, "next year I'm going to be a skeleton like George."

"Oh, honey, that's not a nice costume for a boy your size," Merri protested.

Tim exchanged a look with Mick. It was impatient. Then he patted his mother's arm as though he, not she, were the adult.

"Don't worry, Mum," he said softly. "It'll just be pretend. Underneath, I'll be Tim all the time. Right, Mick?"

"You got it, brother," Mick said.

"Thanks, Mick," said Dad.

He had appeared behind Merri without Mick's being aware of him. And he was grinning at his two sons as though they were his own invention.

Mick was taken aback until he saw, in the eyes so like his own, the love he had almost forgotten in the last months.

Maybe he's like Tim, he thought. Maybe Merri and the divorce and Mum and I have handed him a costume that doesn't feel good but he's stuck with it. Maybe we should let him take it off and be "a person" again.

Embarrassed by his own thoughts, Mick looked away.

"Think nothing of it, Dad," he said. "I always wanted a brother. I admit Tim didn't look promising just at first but he's a great kid underneath."

Then he led the Hallowe'en clown down the hall to the bathtub and turned on the water.

On Seeing a Leaf House

Are small, grave girls still architects with rakes,
Clearing out square, green rooms, piling leaf walls,
Inserting in their proper places doors
And furniture and narrow joining halls?

Those walls were such that any passerby
Could have stepped over them from room to room,
But, when a caller came, she knocked, and I,
Putting by my imaginary broom,

Showed her into the parlour. There we sat
Chatting about the weather, sipping tea,
Admiring the new wallpaper. And if
An uninvited leaf I then should see

Light in the next room, well within arm's reach,
But marring the perfection of the floor,
With what exquisite care I'd rise and go
To fetch it out through the appropriate door.

November

Triolets for Patsy

A triolet's queer.
It looks easy to do;
But that's really unfair
For a triolet's queer.
It rhymes everywhere.
I wrote some for you.
A triolet's queer.
It looks easy to do.

*   *   *

I long for the day
When my sister will come.
We have so much to say.
I long for the day.
She has been far away
But she soon will be home.
I long for the day
When my sister will come.

My sister is here
With her daughter, her son.
It is crowded and queer.
My sister is here
But the hours disappear
And our talk's not begun.
My sister is here
With her daughter, her son.

My sister has gone.
Her visit was good.
It was not like my plan.
My sister has gone
With our talk still undone,
But we loved as we should.
My sister has gone.
Her visit was good.

That our love stay the same
Is the heart of the matter.
I am glad that she came,
That our love stays the same,
Sweet as bread, bright as flame.
We have no need to chatter.
That our love stay the same
Is the heart of the matter.

Now I plan for the day
That waits somewhere ahead.

She has gone far away
But I plan for the day
When she'll come and we'll say
All the things left unsaid.
Now I plan for a day
That waits somewhere ahead.

If these plans go awry,
Still our loving is sure.
Though the hours hurry by,
Though these plans go awry,
We shall laugh, she and I,
And our love will endure.
If these plans go awry,
Still our loving is sure.

I shall write to her now
With my heart in each word.
Of books and the snow
I shall write to her now.
When she reads it, I know
That my love will be heard.
I shall write to her now
With my heart in each word.

1964

Without Beth

Before the twins were born, their parents had an argument.

"If it's a girl, I want to name her Elizabeth after you," their father said.

"Let's not," their mother answered. "Elizabeth the Second! It would sound ridiculous."

When the child turned out to be twin daughters, their father was inspired.

"How about Eliza and Beth?" he suggested.

Their mother laughed and gave in.

Beth was the younger by nine minutes but that was the only time she ever let Eliza get ahead of her. Eliza didn't mind. She liked following Beth. Beth made friends for both of them. Beth chose which game they would play.

"Hide and Seek," she'd call out.

"Good," Eliza would call back. "Beth's It."

Beth named their guinea pigs and dolls. Their favourite dolls were Christmas presents from Great Aunt Emerald the year they were nine. They, too, were identical, but Aunt Emerald had dressed one in red and the other in green.

"How about Holly and Ivy?" Beth asked.

"Perfect," said Eliza. "Mine's Holly."

Beth was the twin most people remembered even though the girls looked so alike, small for their age, with taffy-coloured hair and wide grey-green eyes and dimples.

"Eliza, you're just as smart and pretty as your sister," her anxious parents told her.

"I know," said Eliza. "Stop worrying. I could get along fine without Beth if I had to."

As she said the words, a cold finger of fear touched her. Without Beth. She could not bear to think about her life without her twin. But why should she? They had years to go before they would be grown-up and, even then, they could be near each other. Eliza would see to that.

She liked Beth's games and names. She truly wanted to be the lady-in-waiting and the squire and the enemy and, every so often, the loyal hound. She even enjoyed being Beth's stand-in in school plays and pageants. She had the fun of coming to rehearsals with Mrs. Paganini without ever having to play the parts on stage. She quaked at the very idea of actually speaking lines in front of a live audience. She did not see how Beth could do it.

"It's a good thing I'm healthy, Liza," Beth teased when they were in Grade Seven. "Maybe someday I'll get sick just to see what you'll do."

"Don't," Eliza shivered. "Don't get sick."

The play that year was a comedy about a girl in the olden days who decided to cook an elaborate Christmas dinner for her large family and assorted guests and did everything wrong. Eliza knew all the lines by the second day. She was better at memorizing than her sister. With astonishment, she watched Beth clowning on stage. The play was not all that good. Yet Beth made the mediocre script sparkle. Soon, Eliza was chuckling, and, at the sentimental finish, she was blinking back tears.

Someday Beth will be a famous actress, she thought.

Mrs. Paganini agreed. "This year," she announced, "we're giving two performances. Beth is so good in the main role and people loved her in last year's play. We'll sell tickets and there will be reserved seats. We can donate the money to Famine Relief."

Everyone practised harder than ever. Eliza and Beth were so busy they almost forgot to buy the family tickets. As it was, they got three in one row and one directly behind.

"I'll sit there," Eliza said.

She was excited about seeing the play from out in front. She might be able to concentrate better sitting by herself.

"You'll need new dresses," their mother said. She bought them scarlet jumpers and white silk blouses. They wore them when the family went over to Great

Aunt Emerald's for her birthday dinner in November. Aunt Emerald gave Beth a good luck present. It was a tiny gold star. Beth laughed and pinned it on.

"Is she really a star?" one of their little cousins asked.

"Don't answer that," Beth said. "It might be unlucky to talk about it ahead of time."

"But stars are lucky," the little boy argued. "It'll bring good luck to the person who has it, won't it, Aunt Emerald?"

"That was my intention," his great aunt said.

It did not bring good luck to Beth. The next evening, four days before Opening Night, she grew violently ill. Meningitis. It was a word that would make Eliza shiver even when she was an old woman. Beth seemed fine all day until near suppertime. Then she complained of a bad headache and a stiffness in her neck. Soon she was running a high fever. At nine o'clock, the doctor came. Ten minutes later, an ambulance was at the door. Beth was driven away with sirens screaming. Her voice tight and scared, Mum phoned Aunt Emerald. She gave Eliza a quick hug. Then she and Dad left for the hospital too. Eliza longed to go with them but she didn't ask.

Aunt Emerald came at once by taxi. Eliza wanted to stay up but Aunt Emerald fussed over her so that she finally went to her room. Hers and Beth's.

She got into bed but she could not stay there. She prowled around picking up cassette tapes and books she loved and putting them down again. Even though she did her best to keep her back turned, she kept seeing Beth's empty bed. Finally, she grew so weary she collapsed on the foot of her own bed and dozed. But, even half-asleep, she knew, deep inside herself, that Beth was leaving her. When her father came, at last, to tell her that her sister had died, Eliza hardly heard his words. She was desperately pushing away the very idea of going on without Beth.

"I can't," she whispered. "I don't know how. I can't."

"I know," said her father. But he could not really know. Beth was not his twin. He didn't even have a brother, let alone one who was the other half of himself.

Nobody thought of the school play at first unless it was Mrs. Paganini. She waited a couple of days. Then she came to Eliza's parents. She left it to them to talk with Eliza.

"It is the costume partly," Eliza's mother said. "It is an old-fashioned Victorian dress, as you know. Beth was smaller than the others. It would fit you but it can't be made big enough for anyone else. And Mrs. Paganini says that you know all the lines. Nobody else could memorize them in such a short time."

"Someone else will have to," Eliza said dully. She could not do it and she barely listened.

"The part is too long," her mother said, leaning forward to look into her daughter's wooden face. "It's up to you, dear. Nobody will blame you if you don't do it. But they have advertised and Opening Night is sold out. The money is for Famine—"

"I know about the money," Eliza said stonily.

She couldn't be Beth. She would make a mess of it. There wasn't even time for her to rehearse properly. Her mother left her to think it over. Eliza tried hard not to but finally she gave in. The memory of the starving children she had seen on TV and the thought of the disappointed faces of the cast who had been practising so hard pushed through to her.

"Okay," she growled. "You phone and tell her, though. I can't."

On the night of the play, when Eliza went to dress, she realized for the first time that Mum had taken away all of Beth's clothes. Or she thought she had. When Eliza slid the red jumper over her head and looked in the mirror, she saw, pinned to the front of it, Beth's small gold star.

Her hand reached up and closed on the tiny brooch. Her eyes stung with tears. Then, with trembling fingers, she unfastened it. She was not a star. She knew it and soon everyone else would know too. Yet she did not put the pin in her jewel case or throw it out. She slipped it into her pocket. There was a chance, a small chance, that it would help her get through.

The family drove to the school.

"Would you like me to come with you and help you dress?" Mum asked gently.

Eliza shook her head. She could not trust her voice. She walked to the dressing room feeling like a wind-up toy. She answered "Hi" whenever anyone said "Hi, Eliza." Hardly anyone did. Kids sent her scared glances instead. She put on the long blue gingham dress and, over it, the frilly pinafore. There seemed to be a million tiny buttons and, before she was through, every one of them was slippery with sweat.

At the last moment, she took the tiny pin out of her jumper and slid it into the apron pocket. She was ready.

"As ready as I can be," she told herself. She wondered what would happen if she threw up on stage.

Mrs. Paganini took Eliza's cold hand and squeezed it. "This way, darling," she said, looking as though she were about to burst into tears.

Eliza smiled mechanically, gently disengaged her hand without squeezing back, took a deep breath and followed the teacher onto the stage. Once she got there, she stood stiffly, willing it to be over. Although she did not know it, her face under the make-up was very pale.

"Are you all set?" the teacher asked anxiously.

Eliza nodded her head up and down. Then she walked over to the curtains and parted them slightly. Her right hand dropped to the apron pocket and touched the star. Behind her, Mrs. Paganini blew her nose.

But Eliza did not hear. She was staring through the narrow slit at the rows of people. There were her parents and Great Aunt Emerald. And, in Eliza's empty seat, just behind them, sat her sister Beth.

"It isn't," Eliza breathed and rubbed her eyes.

Beth was still there. She had on a scarlet jumper and white silk blouse. Her eyes were smiling straight at her sister. And, as Eliza stared, she gave the little salute which, between the two of them, had always meant, "Whatever happens, I'm with you."

"Mrs. Paganini," Eliza said hoarsely. "Come and look at the people."

"I know, I know," the teacher said. "It's a full house."

She took Eliza's place, peered out at the audience and smiled broadly.

"They're all rooting for you, sweetheart," she said, turning to pat Eliza's arm. Then she headed for the wings, calling over her shoulder, "Break a leg, honey. Curtain in two minutes."

Eliza laughed softly. She did not look to see if Beth was still there. She moved to the table and took her place, pulling the thick cookbook toward her. As the curtains parted, she pushed back her hair and gave a loud, thoroughly exasperated sigh. The audience laughed in surprise before she had said a word.

Her family were thunderstruck. This vivid, funny girl couldn't be their quiet Eliza. Even though everybody in the auditorium knew about Beth's death, Eliza made them keep chuckling. She played the part almost as Beth would have done. But two or three times she did something Beth had never thought of doing. Every time she did, laughter rang out. Until the final moment. Then she had them in tears.

Eliza got a standing ovation. Smiling and bowing, she knew that she had earned it. Not Beth this time. But Eliza on her own. With Beth watching.

Life still felt grey and empty and there was a long, lonely time in front of her. But Beth would be with her. She knew that now.

Mrs. Paganini's excited voice broke through to her.

"Eliza, you were wonderful," she cried. "I have to confess that I was of two minds as to whether to call the performance off. I didn't know if you could do it without Beth. But you showed us all."

"No," Eliza began. But the teacher didn't hear.

"There was only one empty seat in the whole auditorium," she rushed on. "We'll have a lovely big cheque to send to the Famine Relief fund. Your parents will be so proud."

Eliza did not try to explain again. Mrs. Paganini probably would not believe her. She grinned at the excited teacher and went to change into her regular clothes. When she pulled the scarlet jumper over her head, she took the tiny star pin out of her costume apron and stared down at it. Then she pinned it back onto the jumper where everyone could see it shine.

Halcyon

Alkyone, worn with weeping
For the husband Death had taken,
Feeling by all joy forsaken,
Threw herself into the sea.
As she fell the gods took pity
On the lovely Alkyone
And a kingfisher went winging
Up from where her corpse should be.

When the longest night is over
And the earth turns toward the morning
Of the day that marks the Solstice
And the lengthening of light,
Still a kingfisher goes winging
Out across the wintry ocean
Through the bitter gales, wind-driven,
Seeking somewhere to alight.

Where she comes, the gale grows quiet.
Where she brings her twigs for nesting,
The towering breakers gentle and

Become as frail as foam,
And the bird of myth starts building,
In the wintry waste, oasis,
And she broods upon her nest and makes
The heart of storm her home.

And above that nest the sunlight
Pierces through the tumbling storm clouds,
And reveals the blue of heaven
That glimmers on her wings,
And around the downy fledglings
Comes a lulling of the blizzard
And all are sung to slumber
By the song their mother sings.

And for two whole weeks together,
She charms wind and conjures weather
Till the chicks she hovers over
Hatch and cheep to her for food.
Then she flies off through the darkness
And dives deep into the ocean
And she fishes for her nestlings
And finds nurture for her brood.

Hope is what she comes to show us.
Hope for springtime, hope for healing,
Hope that, after months of winter,
There will be an end to storm.
She comes not to help us idle

In the torpid tropic breezes
But to let us glimpse a wonder,
A swift memory of warm.

When you read those tracts for tourists
That prate of "halcyon havens,"
Recall that glimpse of azure
Is not really meant to last.
It is but a breath, a promise,
That grief, in time, will gentle,
That, if we wait, the cold within
Will break and bloom at last.

According to Webster's Dictionary of Word Origins, 1991, the word "halcyon" stems from a Greek legend. Alkyone, daughter of Aeolus, god of the winds, was so griefstricken on learning her husband had been drowned that she attempted to throw herself into the sea. The gods pitied her and transformed her into a kingfisher. This bird nested on the ocean and, while her eggs were incubated, the wind was gentle and the weather warm.

December

The Question of Christmas

Can the Christ Child find a home
With cherubs made of styrofoam;
Where P.A. systems make a blight
Of "Silent Night, Holy Night";
Where the Star that tops the tree
Blinks on and off electrically;
Where people unpack and assemble
Pseudo-trees they claim resemble
Spruce and pine except that they
Stay tidy, can be stored away,
Shed no needles, smell so dull,
Hygienic, economical—
And here's a spray that smells like pine,
A bargain at two ninety-nine?

What of the Super Funtime toys
We're urged to give our girls and boys:
Svelte fashion dolls who style their hair,
Have closets full of clothes to wear,
On whom a fortune must be spent
To keep their lifestyle affluent?

They've knowing eyes and legs like giraffes
And buxom busts and, just for laughs,
Their wedding gowns and their bikinis,
To be put on, require Houdinis.
Mothers across the land, take warning.
You'll dress that doll all Christmas morning
And undress her all afternoon.
It's Christmas. You can't swear or swoon.
Just watch your fingernails get mangled
While her smooth fall of hair grows tangled.

Or watch instead your small boy's fun
Playing so nicely with that gun.
He now has all he needs, and more
To work the magic game called War,
—Bombs, bazookas and—Oh, brother!—
Some little men to slay each other!
If you're a pacifist, why not
Get a slime pit for your tot?
Instead of that old-fashioned sled,
Buy him a vampire for his bed
Or perhaps he'd rather cuddle up
With an almost lifelike pup
Which yaps and yips unceasingly
And, best of all, can poop and pee . . .
Batteries not included though
So you can't get the thing to go.
Did three Kings come to Bethlehem?
Zeller's has a gross of them.

Ninety-nine cents each they are,
Cardboard stable, punch-out star.
Sham fireplaces cleanly glow
And you can get synthetic snow,
Red-nosed reindeer, plastic holly . . .
And "Ho, ho, ho!" obesely jolly
Omnipresent Santas loom
From wide screens in the living room,
At Shopping Plazas by the score . . .

Oh, what is all the falseness for?
Must Christmas be so loud, so neat,
New, Improved and sticky sweet,
Too much to give, too much to take,
A gaily gift-wrapped, festive fake?
Where is the pain of Christmas night,
Joseph's worry, Mary's fright?
Where the truth within the story,
The hurt, the tenderness, the glory?
Today we're standing in the inn,
Lost in the crowd, tired of the din.
Let us go out into the dark
And, in the blessed silence, hark!
A woman singing, "Lullaby,"
The stir of beasts, a baby's cry.
While we are yet aware, still able,
Let us go out and find the stable.

The Portable Christmas

The Penny twins were the last to leave the warm classroom. The other kids were almost out of sight when Nick pulled shut the door of the portable. He jumped the steps and headed for home.

Holly slipped on the icy second step and almost fell flat on her face in the wet snow. She waved her arms, regained her balance, made it safely to the ground and gave the portable a baleful backward glance.

"I hate portables," she muttered. "Everything in our lives is portable now, Nick. Did you realize that?"

Her brother slowed down until she was at his side. He did not ask her what she was going on about. He knew. He also knew he had better let her get it out of her system or she'd go on grumping and groaning all the way home.

"Ever since Mum and Dad got divorced," she said, "we've had to pack up every other second and go somewhere else. One week here, one week there. I know—they gave that up. But I hate moving every other weekend too. The stuff I need is always at the other place. And Christmas is awful. Remember last year?"

Nick did remember. He grimaced but did not interrupt her.

"We had to move around all day long. Get up and open presents at Mum's. Leave those gifts behind. Get picked up and open more presents at Dad's. Leave the new stuff behind even if it was a book or a game. Then drive to Grandpa and Grandma's and open more. Stick those in a bag to take home to Mum's. And then go all the way out to the country to see Great Grandpa and . . ."

"I remember," Nick broke in at last. "I was there too. It was not the best Christmas ever. But we're stuck with it. It'll be the same this year except for everyone making even more fuss over the Revolting Child otherwise known as Baby Susie."

"You know what, Nick, Dad should have called her Mistletoe if he wanted her to fit in and be our true baby sister. We could call her Mistletoe," Holly's voice was high and a little shrill.

"No, we couldn't. She wasn't born on December 25th," Nick said mildly. "She's only a baby. She'll probably improve."

"Don't count on it," Holly said, kicking at an inoffensive treetrunk which was near the sidewalk. "But it's not really Susie that makes everything so disgusting. It's the way we don't matter any longer. We're like parcels. They can't leave us behind but they never bother to open us and see what's inside."

They trudged on in silence for a couple of blocks. Then Holly burst into speech once again.

"We shouldn't have been born on Christmas," she fumed. "Why did we rush like that? We could have been born in February if we'd just hung on."

Nick laughed.

"With our luck, it would have been February 14th and Mum would have named us Cupid and Valentina," he snorted.

Holly had to laugh too. But there was misery just under the laughter. Their parents' divorce had made everything harder but their Christmassy names had been a burden from the day their Grade One teacher, Miss Brigson, had gushed about them in front of the whole class.

A far-off voice chanted,

> Prickle and Nickel
> Are sour as a pickle.

The twins did not even look around. They were used to being called names. They had had five Christmas seasons of it by now.

"If only Miss Brigson hadn't noticed," Holly said again.

"Yeah," Nick said.

Holly almost always talked for both of them. It was one of the things that drove their stepmother crazy.

"Why, your birthday is December 25th," Miss Brigson had said in a voice that carried to every corner of the classroom. "Your mother must have been thrilled to have twins for Christmas. A double present. I should have noticed your names. Holly Carol and Nicholas Noel. How sweet!"

They had not looked at each other but their hearts had plummeted into their shoes. All they could do was hope that the kids would have forgotten before December arrived. They hadn't.

Then, to top it off, Miss Brigson had made things worse by loving the carols which Holly and Nick had grown to loathe.

"The holly bears a prickle," she had taught the class, "As sharp as any thorn . . ."

The kids grinned even as they sang. The twins had been Prickle and Nickel from that day on. What did all of it matter? Christmas was coming and they had to get through it. Another portable Christmas.

"We should go on strike or something," Nick said idly.

And, right then, Holly had her magnificent idea. She opened her mouth to blurt it out and then made herself wait until she thought. She had to work out the details. If she were to get Nick to go along with her, she had to think of every possible snag.

By Christmas Eve, they had perfected each detail of the plan. Nick had been persuaded without too much trouble. Holly went to bed feeling sick to her stomach with excitement. If only Nick didn't chicken out at the last minute and refuse to come!

She had her little alarm clock under her pillow but

she did not need it to ring. She felt as though she had not slept at all and, at four o'clock, she eased out of bed and crept into Nick's room. To her astonishment, he was sleeping soundly. She put her hand over his mouth to rouse him. His eyes flew open at once.

"Come on," she breathed.

He slid out of bed. He was already dressed. They had put their clothes back on the minute Mum had left their rooms the night before. Holly knelt to get the gym bag out from under his bed. They tiptoed downstairs and made for the front door.

Then Nick remembered the note.

Holly went back and put it on the mantel above the fake fireplace. Mum would spot it eventually. It was in a small, plain envelope so it might not catch her eye for a while. That suited the twins. The scariest part was unlocking the front door and shutting it again without making a betraying click.

"This is the first time in my life that I've been glad we don't have a dog," Nick whispered.

They tiptoed down the drive past the other townhouses and then, feeling safe at last, they ran. The snow had melted days ago. It was going to be what people called "a green Christmas" although the twins saw nothing green about it. All the visible grass was brown and dead looking. Who cared? They walked to the bus stop and waited.

"Maybe it won't be running on Christmas," Nick said.

"It will," Holly said. "I checked. We're just early."

Finally, before it was fully light, the bus pulled up. The children climbed on and said "Merry Christmas" to the driver.

"Where are you two bound? Do your parents know you're out?" he questioned.

"Of course they do. They arranged for us to go to our grandfather's," Holly said, gazing at him with her innocent eyes. Nick, who was a transparent liar, kept his head down and his mouth shut.

They took the subway after that and then the Greyhound bus from the terminal. Once they were seated near the back and nobody seemed to be noticing them, Holly slumped down in relief and fell asleep. Nick was the one who watched, afraid they would fail to get off in Guelph. It seemed to take forever. He kept thinking of his mother's face as she read Holly's note.

She had written:

> Mum,
>
> We are not parcels. We are people. We have gone to a peaceful place. When Dad comes to Great Grandpa's, we'll be there and he can bring us home. We'll open our presents with you tomorrow. Today is our birthday and we don't want to spend it being moved around.
>
> Love,
> Holly and Nick

Nick wondered what Mum would do. Would she understand? How much trouble were they going to be in?

Then the bus turned off to Guelph and Nick woke his sister. There was no point in worrying. If you were having an adventure, have an adventure.

The trickiest part was phoning Great Grandpa from the bus terminal. Holly would do the talking, of course, but Nick pressed close to give her courage.

"Michael Benson here," Great Grandpa said.

"Hi," Holly began, her voice faint and quavering.

"Who is it?" His tone was sharp.

She suddenly could not go on. After a moment, Nick grabbed the receiver, afraid Great Grandpa would hang up.

"It's us, Nick and Holly," he shouted into the phone. "We're at the Guelph bus station. Can you come and get us?"

There was an interminable silence. Then Great Grandpa gave a bark of what might have been laughter or might have been a growl.

"I'll be there in ten minutes," he said, and hung up.

The twins sagged with relief. They had to hold each other up. Then they went and sat on a bench to wait.

The jeep pulled up outside the terminal in twelve minutes. Great Grandpa got out and looked at the door of the building. Holly and Nick had been watching and he had no need to fetch them. They were running toward him as though he were Santa Claus himself. He hugged them close. It was the most comforting hug they had had in a long time.

"Happy Birthday, children. Pile in," he said. "You can tell me all about it on the way to the farm."

Holly, her courage completely recovered, told him. He had already guessed most of it. He had seen, the previous Christmas, how sullen and weary the kids looked, not like children who were having a birthday and Christmas rolled into one. He had wanted to help but had not been allowed to. He was their great-grandfather and, although he had just turned eighty, his children and grandchildren had kept telling him to sit down and take it easy as though he were worn out.

This was the first time, since they were born, that he had ever been completely alone with Nick and Holly for more than five minutes. He decided to make the most of it.

He did not mention the frantic phone calls, his granddaughter-in-law in near hysterics, his grandson terse and very angry at having his Christmas spoiled by the twins. Susie, an over-indulged child if Great Grandpa had ever seen one, was shrieking in the background and, for the first time in her short life, being ignored. He hoped it did her good.

He had promised to call if he heard anything. He had not promised to call at once. He would let them stew a while. He wanted to spend some uninterrupted time with these brave and resourceful children.

The three of them had a sumptuous breakfast. Mary,

his daughter, who had married a farmer and lived on the next concession, had left him plentifully supplied with food. She always gave him too much. But he ignored the fancy coffee cake she had baked and fried up eggs, bacon and onions. He cut big slices of the homemade loaf another neighbour had given him and slathered them with butter and honey from his own bees. Holly and Nick gulped it all down as though they were starving. When they were stuffed to the eyebrows, they groaned and sat back.

"Now get your duds on," he told them. "I have a cow who's calving. She might have managed alone. But I don't think so. I was with her when you called. I have a phone in the barn now."

As they hiked out to the barn, a few first snowflakes began drifting lazily down. The wind sighed through the evergreen trees.

> ... the only other sound's the sweep
> Of easy wind and downy flake ...

Great Grandpa quoted.

Holly looked at him, puzzled.

"I know that . . ." she said uncertainly.

He recited the whole poem. Her face lit up.

"We have it in our reader," she said.

"It's how I feel here," Nick said dreamily. "I never want to go back."

"You will," Great Grandpa said.

Bess, the cow, was giving birth as they came in. It was the most exciting thing the Pennys had ever witnessed. And it went on because she had a second calf a few minutes later. Twins!

"You could call them Holly and Nick," Holly said.

"I could if they weren't both heifers," Great Grandpa chuckled.

Once the twin calves were standing up tipsily on their long, spindly legs and having breakfast, Great Grandpa sent the children to collect some evergreen boughs and made the promised phone call. There was great jubilation in faraway Toronto.

"Just wait till I get my hands on them," Michael Benson's grandson said, remembering belatedly to be angry.

Then his grandfather delivered himself of a few pithy remarks about how the children had had to run away to find a proper Christmas, and the younger man was silent.

They all arrived in mid-afternoon, the twins' grandparents, Mary and her husband George, and their daughter Eleanor, Mum, Dad and his wife and little Susie. As they drove in, more snowflakes came spinning down from the dark sky. They had come laden with Christmas fare. Everyone was in the same house and nobody needed to go anywhere. The presents were opened and there was time to play with them while the adults talked and sorted out the various dishes they had brought for the Christmas feast.

After the eating was over, Grandma went to the piano and they sang carols. Susie, snuggled in her father's arms, slept peacefully. Everyone smiled at her whenever a sleeping baby was mentioned. When, at last, it was time to go, Dad walked a heavy-eyed Nick and a yawning Holly out to Mum's car and tucked them in. They were asleep instantly.

"They had the right idea all along," he said gently, grinning at the children who, even in their sleep, were clutching their presents from Great Grandpa.

"I loved it," their mother said. "It was real, wasn't it? Not a dream?"

"It was real," he answered, smiling at her now.

"Next year, let's all start out here," Great Grandpa's voice said, quiet and deep. "I've got room for all of you."

"But Grandpa, you're eighty . . ." somebody said.

"So next year, I'll be eighty-one," Great Grandpa said cheerfully. "But not, I think, dead. If I am, you can make other plans. But get together. Don't drag the children from pillar to post."

One by one, the cars pulled away into the snowy night. Great Grandpa went out to check on Bess and her twins.

"I'm going to call you Happy and Birthday," he told them.

Bess lowed softly.

He rubbed the top of her head and stood regarding the sleeping twin calves.

"Next year," he said to her, "I'll invite the twins to come a day ahead. Next year, they won't have to run away to find Christmas. It will be here waiting."

The Little Brown Calf

The little brown calf was born that night.
Sticky and new, he lay in the stall,
Sprawled in a shaft of ruddy light
That fell from a lantern on the wall.

At last, he cocked up one knobbly leg,
Struggled to stand and—tipped on his nose!
Struggled and heaved again until,
Tottering, swaying still, he rose.

He stood there, balancing, all alone,
His four hooves widely braced on the ground,
And, letting his mother lick him clean,
He took his first big-eyed look around.

He peered down dizzily at his stall.
Then, ducking his mother's swabbing tongue,
He peeked at the stall across from his
And there was a creature equally young.

They stared at each other and, all at once,
Each found a friend in that alien place.
The little brown scrap of a calf stood still
Gazing down on the small, loved face.

The great cows creaked to their knees, but he
Stayed erect, to his own surprise.
And the angels hushed while calf and child
Remembered together Paradise.

They Needed a Midwife

My mother delivered
   that baby at the inn
And my mother stormed,
   "It's a shame and a sin
For a babe to be born
   in a barn like that.
Every time I stirred,
   I stepped on the cat!
And that girl was in labour
   in an open stall,
With stable boys gawking
   and pigeons and all."

"Well," drawled my father,
   "many a cow
Has let down her calf
   in that stall before now."

My mother looked daggers
   and her cheeks went red.

"Oh, men make me sick!"
   my good mother said.
"That Caesar's another!
   I call it a crime
When a woman has to travel
   so close to her time.
She was white as a curd
   before we were done
Though she roused and she glowed
   when I showed her her son."

"Well," smiled my father,
   "didn't you too
When your first manchild
   was brought to you?"

"This one's sweet," Mother murmured,
   "so cunning and strong.
But people kept bothering us
   all night long.
Three foreigners barged in
   from who knows where
And some shepherds from the hill-fold
   burst in there,
Keeping him awake and
   wearying her
With presents of new lambs
   and incense and myrrh."

"Presents?" asked my father,
    "For a child like that?
Didn't you say he's
    some carpenter's brat?"

"The strangers," Mother answered,
    "had journeyed far.
They said God guided them
    with a star!
And those shepherds claimed they'd
    heard angels sing,
'Unto you this night
    is born a king!'
He might be the Messiah,
    so one of them said.
And I laid him in a manger
    for want of a bed."

"The Messiah!" scoffed my father.
    "A king! My word,
That's the greatest nonsense
    I ever heard."

My mother, who uses
    more words than a book,
Sat silent a moment
    and wore a queer look.
"He's such a bonny baby,"
    she said then, low.

"I washed him and dressed him.
   How are we to know?
I sang him a cradle song,
   the poor little scrap.
Suppose I was holding
   a king on my lap."

A Mantle of Praise

"If you can spare me, mistress, I want to go home with Jacob when he goes to be registered for the tax," Susannah said that Sabbath morning.

Ruth's eyes widened and her breath caught in her throat. Susannah couldn't be going away and leaving her here alone with Grandmother!

The older woman stiffened and her voice, when it came, grated harshly.

"There's no need for you to go. Only men are required to journey to their birthplaces and be counted. You'll just be in the way. As I'm sure Jacob has told you, I'll have need of you right here taking care of . . . things."

Ruth flinched. She knew what her grandmother meant. She was one of the chief "things" Susannah took care of. From the day Ruth, a tiny baby, had been unceremoniously dropped off at the house in Bethlehem, Ruth's grandmother had had no time or attention to spare for the child. She never struck her, but she spoke sharply or kept a cold silence when Ruth was needing attention. Before the child was old enough to talk clearly and walk about without losing her balance, she had started hiding behind Susannah's wide skirts whenever her grandmother was home. Susannah's warm, bulky person had been a sanctuary for her. Her shield and buckler, that was what Susannah was. And Susannah knew Ruth's need of her.

"I'm sorry, mistress," Susannah said, her voice respectful but stubborn. "I've had word that my sister is very ill and who knows but this may be my last chance to see her. I haven't been home for almost ten years, you must remember."

Ruth had never thought about Susannah having a home somewhere away from Bethlehem. Once in a while, the maidservant had mentioned her younger sister and Jacob's two brothers but they had always seemed like half-legendary children who had their place in stories of long ago and far away, not like living grown-up people with homes of their own in a small town on the other side of Jerusalem. Ruth and her grandparents had seemed to be Susannah's and Jacob's people. The idea of Susannah departing even for a few days was unthinkable.

In all her nine years of life, Ruth had never had to spend more than an hour or two alone with her mother's mother or with the hardworking, mostly silent man who was her grandfather. Always Susannah had been there to put her to bed and get her up and dressed and see to it that she ate. When she had been a little thing and cried, Susannah had comforted her.

Hush, little chicken.
Don't wake up the house.
Curl up and sleep again,
Snug as a mouse.

She had crooned under her breath so as not to waken the older couple. Ruth had known enough to whisper her wants or her nightmares. When she had needed to know something, she had always gone straight to Susannah. The servant had often been impatient but Ruth had understood that, beneath the tart words and huffy sighs, there was a friend she could trust. Susannah had even risked Grandmother's fierce anger more than once for Ruth's sake.

Most startling of all had been the day she had secretly given Ruth her mother's white mantle with its wide blue border.

Long ago Grandmother had ordered Susannah to burn it but the serving woman had hidden it instead until Ruth was seven. Then, when Grandmother was delivering a baby on the far side of the village, the maidservant had brought out the length of cloth wrapped in a piece of coarse sheeting.

"When your mother was planning to marry, she wove this," she told Ruth in a whisper. "She said that she was going to wear it at her wedding. I had no idea she had her plans laid already to wed a Roman. After your great-grandfather found out about him and forbade her to meet him again, she ran off. The old man died six weeks later and your grandmother thought Deborah's running off brought on his stroke. Then, when a year went by and your father's people sent you here in a servant's care, you came wrapped in it. Your mother had died. There was no other message except that your father was also dead and his family refused to take responsibility for you.

Ruth made a small sound of protest and Susannah's words swept on.

"I don't believe your father had died. The man wouldn't look me in the eye when he said the words. Your grandmother swallowed it all, even the bit about no proper marriage ceremony, and said that I should destroy the mantle, but it's beautiful and your mother wove it herself when she was happy. I thought you should have it. You have little enough of hers. Only this piece of cloth and those great round eyes of yours."

"What did she look like?" Ruth began eagerly. "Were her eyes really like mine?"

"Now don't start in on a string of questions! I was told never to speak of her again and I promised. You just tuck this away where nobody will find it and, when you're a grown woman, you can wear it. And think of her kindly. She was a lovely warm-hearted girl and all the joy went out of this house the day she ran off."

Watching Susannah starting to pack her few clothes, Ruth remembered the words and felt her cheeks grow hot. If Grandmother knew what she kept folded flat under her pallet bed, what would she do?

The girl jerked her thoughts away from the very idea in case her grandmother could somehow read her mind. Until five minutes ago, she had known that, if her grandmother found out, Susannah would stand like a protecting wall between her and the storm which would surely break over her head. Yet if, while Susannah was gone, Grandmother looked under the pallet . . . !

Grandmother had hired both Jacob and his wife only a few weeks before Deborah's going. When the baby Ruth had been brought to the house, perhaps Susannah had been dismayed at being required to take on the care of a sickly infant. But unlike her mistress, she had felt her heart go out to the puny child. Susannah had found her a wet nurse and, from that day to this, all the little girl knew of love had been taught her by the two servants.

Ruth had known for years that her grandmother did not want her.

"She should never have been born," she had overheard her say once.

"Be still, Dorcas. She'll hear you," Grandfather had muttered, casting a swift, anxious look over his shoulder to where Ruth stood in the shadowed doorway gazing out at a band of children playing in the street.

Until he spoke, Ruth had not realized that the bitter words referred to herself. Yet her grandmother's outburst had not told the child anything she had not guessed long since. How could she fail to notice that her mother's mother seldom spoke to her directly and never touched her if she could help it?

By now, the distance between them was accepted by both as normal. Instead of fighting to win the love of her stern grandparents, Ruth had turned herself into a shadow, small and silent, who kept out of everyone's way. Ruth also knew that her grandmother wanted her to keep out of sight when neighbours came to the house.

If Martha from next door or Abigail from across the road dropped in to borrow something or to gossip, her grandmother always sent Ruth into another room. After a while, she disappeared from sight the moment she heard footsteps approaching.

Once she had dared to ask Susannah why her grandmother hated her. Susannah had reddened and refused to meet Ruth's eyes.

"It's not that. She just isn't fond of children, that's all. It has nothing to do with you," the maid had mumbled. "Now bring me a measure of barley and leave me to get on with my work."

Ruth had gone for the barley but, once she had handed it over, she had said stubbornly, "You know she doesn't want me. I even heard her say so. She's ashamed of me. Why? Did she hate my mother too?"

"Your mother was the light of her life," Susannah answered slowly, as though she were speaking against her will. "If your mother had only stayed home and married someone we all knew . . . But no use weeping over what's broken and can't be mended. Just take it from me that life has not been easy for her."

"But, Susannah," Ruth began to argue.

"She likes you well enough, child. She's given you a home all these years, hasn't she? She's been kind to Jacob and me and kept us on even when times were hard. Run along, do. I can't concentrate with you pestering me."

Ruth had run from the room, frightened that she might lose the quick-tempered but steady tenderness the maid gave her. She suspected that her grandfather liked her better than her grandmother did, but he was so taciturn that she was not entirely sure she was right.

Jacob and she were good friends, but Jacob was mostly outside or in the shop hard at work. Her grandfather owned the village carpentry shop and also had a small flock of sheep in a fold in the nearby hills. Jacob, with a boy to help, watched over the sheep. Both men worked long hours and had little time to spend on household matters.

After talking with Susannah about Grandmother, Ruth went out behind the house to the three olive trees that grew crookedly together and formed a private place which she had claimed as her own. Crouching down in their shadow, she pondered what the maidservant had let slip but she did not feel much wiser. Although Susannah claimed that Grandmother was not fond of children and Ruth could not remember a time when a child had been invited into the house, something told the little girl that Susannah's excuse was not the whole story. After all, Grandmother knew the name of every boy and girl for miles around. She had brought most of them into the world and she had gone to help nurse many through frightening bouts of fever. When Bethlehem children were ill, she was the first one summoned and she often remained over a night or two. She spoke of them in a dry way, it was true, but never with the bitterness she saved for Ruth. And she never, ever said Ruth's name.

Once or twice, Ruth thought this was about to change. She would look up from her quiet play in time to see the start of a smile tugging at Grandmother's set mouth. Then, when she caught Ruth's gaze, her mother's mother would gasp, as though something had hurt her. The next instant, she would be so cold and withdrawn that Ruth had to believe she had imagined the whole thing.

"It is time the child was in bed," she would say brusquely. Or, "Put that down, girl, and go help Susannah."

Surely Susannah would not abandon her, even to see her sister! Or she might offer to take Ruth along . . .

But neither of these things happened. Jacob and his wife quietly and obstinately stuck to their plan and at last Ruth's grandmother had no choice but to give in.

"If you don't," Ruth heard her grandfather saying in the night, "they may leave us even after all these years. I need Jacob. I'd never find another man who would do his work as faithfully. Let them go, Dorcas. You can look after the child. She's old enough to take care of herself for that matter. She's quick and smart like Deborah."

"Don't," her grandmother cried. "She's a timid little thing, always running to Susannah. Deborah, whatever her faults, had courage and wit. Comparing them is like saying a lion cub and a mouse are twin souls."

"Her name is Ruth," her grandfather said in the darkness. "We've never let her be a lion cub."

Ruth waited, every nerve taut. Her grandmother did not answer.

When the servants set out down the road the following morning, Susannah riding one of Grandfather's two donkeys and Jacob trudging along at its head, Ruth stood in the street for all to behold and waved until they were out of sight. Even when she could no longer see them growing smaller and smaller in the dusty distance, she continued to stare after them.

Grandmother had come out to say goodbye but had gone back in before they had passed the tree which grew where their property joined Simon and Martha's. Ruth half-turned and peered at the open doorway. Her grandfather was standing there watching her with understanding eyes.

"They'll soon be home, girl," he said gruffly. "Come in now."

Ruth, surprised and wary, did as she was told. If he would stay with them, things would be easier. Perhaps

94

he had guessed as much and would not go to the shop for a bit. At first, she thought he had read her mind. But her grandmother, seeing him lingering, said tartly, "If you've nothing better to do, Isaac, you might take this herbal remedy across to Aaron's. His wife told me he has been having trouble sleeping because of pains in his chest."

Her grandfather took the clay bottle and went out without looking at Ruth. She must have imagined that gentleness she thought she had seen.

It was a silent house all afternoon. When Grand-mother needed Ruth's help, which she seldom did, she did not need to ask or explain, for Ruth was watching out for such moments and did what she had often seen Susannah do. Even so, she could tell that her grand-mother was as relieved as she was when Grandfather came in for his evening meal. The tension slackened the minute he stepped through the door.

Ruth retired to her pallet bed early, glad to close her eyes and pretend to be asleep. She thought of the soft white and blue mantle which lay hidden beneath her pallet and she felt stronger. The time would pass. A whole day had gone by already. She lay trying to count the hours until Susannah would return and life would be normal again.

The night felt strange. The absence of the servants was not all that made it different. There were crowds in the street. Shouts rang out. Animals brayed. A woman laughed excitedly in a nearby house. Ruth even heard children run past, long after all Bethlehem youngsters were usually sent to their beds. Scores of visitors had come to town because of the Roman Emperor's decree that every man should return to his birthplace to be registered in the Imperial census. Once this had been accomplished, the tax gatherers would know where to go for their money.

Ruth longed to go out and see what was happening. After all, if she had it right, her father was a Roman soldier. She turned over restlessly. Why had he sent her away when her mother died? If he was alive, why didn't he ever come to see her? And if, someday, by some tremendous luck, he should come . . . would he, too, think her a mouse not worth bothering with?

Who had named her Ruth? She did not even know that. Susannah did not know either. Ruth had asked her often for any detail about the man who had become her father but the servant had grown so agitated each time that at last Ruth had promised to stop asking.

She could not stop wondering, though. Every day, almost every hour, she wondered. It gnawed at her like a secret hunger. Deep within her was the conviction that something was wrong with her that kept him from coming or even sending a messenger to ask about her. Whatever it was, it was something so terrible that nobody would tell her, knowing it would wound her deeply.

But what?

She was small, she knew, and homely maybe.

Her mother had been beautiful and, one afternoon when she had been sure that her grandmother would not come home and catch her, Ruth had gotten out the mantle and put it over her own head. Susannah, coming back from the well, had gasped when she saw her and sat down heavily. But what Ruth remembered best was her exclamation.

"Oh, child, you look the image of your mother! Those are her very eyes looking out of your face. Put the mantle away. Your grandmother must never see you like that."

If her mother had beautiful eyes and hers were so like them, didn't that mean her eyes must be beautiful too? Ruth wondered for the hundredth time. They were very big, she knew, and although they were brown, they had golden glints which made them different. Her grandmother and grandfather and Susannah and Jacob all had brown eyes, too, but theirs were dark.

"It's a wild night, this," she heard Grandfather saying. "There's not an empty bed in town. There have already been a couple of battles at the inn. And having soldiers here to help keep things in order isn't helping."

"It wouldn't," Grandmother snorted. She had no use for Roman soldiers. "I only hope that Simon's wife doesn't decide to have her baby before morning. I saw her sister at the well and she said there was no sign of . . ."

"Goodwife Dorcas," a voice called from outside the house. "Is she there? She's needed."

97

Grandmother hurried to the door. "Is it Anna?" she began.

"No, mistress," the deep voice explained with a rough laugh. "It's one of the wayfarers who've come to be counted. The fool man brought his young wife and she's started her pains."

Ruth lay still, her heart thudding. What would happen now? Would her grandfather offer to stay with her? He usually went back to his shop in the early evening.

"Dorcas, you'll have to take Ruth with you. She won't be in the way. She's so small and silent I sometimes wonder if Deborah gave birth to a ghost."

"She's only nine, not big enough to be any help. What if she swoons or some such thing? I can go and be back before she wakes."

Ruth held her breath and waited. She was afraid to be left alone in the house.

"I can't stay. I promised Elihu to help out down at the inn. Their stables are full of beasts. Where this baby will be born I can't think. Ruth's intelligent, though you may never have noticed. Just sit her out of the way and tell her to keep still till you're done. We can't leave her by herself here, not with the crowds in the street. Even if no harm came to her, she would waken and be afraid."

Ruth thought she had never heard her grandfather make such a long speech. Perhaps he loved her after all. Footsteps approached her corner. She lay still and kept her eyes closed. Grandmother shook her shoulder.

"Wake up, girl. I'm needed. You'll have to come along but keep out of the way. Get dressed. You can carry this."

As Ruth scrambled into her clothes, her grandmother put things into two baskets. As soon as she saw Ruth was waiting, she handed the smaller one to her.

"Now you stick to me like a burr," she instructed. "There are rough people in the streets and men may shout at us. Ignore them and follow close behind me. We just have to go to the stable behind the inn. If you stay close, you'll be perfectly safe."

They had to push their way through a throng of men and animals. Ruth started out at her grandmother's side. She had to run a few steps every so often to keep up but they had gone halfway before anything went amiss. Then, with no warning at all, Ruth found herself jostled and shoved to the edge of the road.

"Grandmother!" she called in panic.

She had never used that word before but her grandmother did not question it. She sprang swift as a lioness to rescue Ruth, sweeping her close with one strong arm and tucking her in behind her back.

"Hold onto my clothes and stay close, Ruth," she ordered. "I'll make a path for you. I'm glad you called out or I might have lost you."

The little girl, clutching the edge of her grandmother's mantle, was astonished.

Ruth! Her grandmother had called her Ruth. And she had said she was glad not to have lost her. Didn't she want to be rid of her? Sticking so close that she trod twice on her grandmother's heels, Ruth longed for peace and quiet so that she could think. She had called out "Grandmother" and her grandmother had actually sprung to save her.

"Here we are," said Grandmother, turning into the alleyway that led to the back of the inn. "I can't think what they meant saying I was to come to the stable. Isaac should be here before us. Perhaps he knows something."

"There he is," Ruth said. "Look."

Grandfather hurried toward them. He wasn't coming from the stable where guests lodged their animals but from a tumbledown cow byre at the very back of the property. Light spilled through the open doorway.

"This way, Dorcas," he called. "They've put her out here. Benjamin claims he hasn't a bed to spare inside and he's being kind to give them shelter at all with the woman about to give birth, but how you'll manage in that hovel is anyone's guess. It's cramped and none too clean. Here, let me take that. I'll get you settled before I go to help out with the horses and mules. There are even some camels!"

Grandmother handed over her basket and Ruth's smaller one. As she shifted it, she took Ruth's hand in hers, almost as though she were unaware of what she was doing, and led her across the rough earth. Grandfather had to duck his head as the three of them entered through the low door.

"Oh, my soul, what a place to be having a baby!" Grandmother exclaimed. She dropped Ruth's hand and hurried to the heap of hay where a young woman lay, her face glistening with sweat, her eyes frightened.

"Don't you be afraid, my poor girl," Ruth heard the voice, usually so stern, crooning.

Then Grandmother, moving like lightning, set about unpacking the things she had brought. First she gave the young woman something to drink which seemed to steady her. Then she caught a stable boy peering in through the door and sent him to fetch hot water. She tore up pieces of cloth into towels.

Ruth watched the hasty preparations with wide eyes. She still stood near the door and she felt small and useless. Her grandfather had vanished.

"Ruth," her grandmother called. "come here to me."

Ruth, wide-eyed at hearing her own name spoken so calmly, obeyed.

"This is going to take a while," Grandmother said in a low voice meant for Ruth's ears alone. "I want you to make ready a bed for the infant so we'll have a place to put it when it comes. Use . . . use one of those mangers. That empty one. Find hay and pad it thickly. I'd give you some cloth but I'm going to need all I've brought. Can you manage?"

"Yes," Ruth said doubtfully, gazing at the rough wooden manger which looked like nothing more or less than a large, splintery box with cracks in it. How could she make such a thing into a baby's bed?

But she must. She did not want the baby to arrive and find nobody had made a place for it. She started carrying handfuls of straw and dropping them in. It was going to take far too long.

A man rushed in, banging his head on the low lintel as he did so. He ignored Ruth and her grandmother completely and hurried over to where the woman lay moaning softly.

"I paid him, Mary," he told her. "The minute somebody vacates a room, he has promised to move you into it. If you could just hang on a few hours longer . . ."

"She'll do nothing of the kind, young man," Grandmother said. "This child is in a hurry to get here. He'll arrive in an hour or two at the most. Fork some hay into that manger so that my granddaughter can make it into a bed."

The woman laughed weakly.

"I'm all right, Joseph, now that the midwife has come," she said, her voice loving but thin with weariness. "Do help the little girl. She shouldn't be here . . ."

"Nonsense," Ruth's grandmother said. "She has to start learning sometime. I do believe she's going to be a help. Go and fork some hay, Joseph."

Joseph did, but he was not really paying attention. Half the forkload landed on the floor. Then he was gone back to his wife. Ruth scooped the scattered hay up and patted it down into the manger. It made a soft enough bed. Her own pallet at home was filled with hay. But all the loose ends would prickle and scratch a baby. She needed a length of soft cloth.

My mantle, she thought. My mantle would be perfect.

But it was back at the house. It was not so far if the way were not so crowded. Maybe if she took the back alley and kept out of sight . . .

Ruth was so afraid that she almost did not go. Then she remembered Grandmother saying she was a mouse and thought about the baby being dumped into that prickly bed with its none too clean hay. She went silently out of the cow byre and slipped along back of the inn through the inky black shadows.

They were so busy bringing that baby along that she would not be missed for ten or fifteen minutes. That was time enough if all went well. She was astonished to find herself at their back door in no time. She was so small and she had flitted so stealthily from shadow to shadow that nobody had noticed her. She got into the house without trouble and ran straight to her pallet. The mantle was there, soft as down, white as snow. Now all she had to do was go back.

She stood just inside the door, listening. She had blown out the lamp and the room was dark. Yet the night that waited beyond the door loomed darker than that within the familiar room. Still, she must go. At any moment, her grandmother was going to look around for her. She hugged the bundled-up mantle against her chest and put her free hand out to draw back the bar that held the door shut. Her fingers were icy cold. She could feel them trembling.

Susannah, cried a small voice inside her.

Then she had an idea. She shook out the mantle and caught a white glimmer even in the darkness. Then she wrapped it around her face and clutched its folds together beneath her chin. She looked like her mother in it. Susannah had said so. And her mother had been brave enough to run away from home to marry a soldier.

As she darted along in the deep shadows next to the road, it may have been the whiteness of her mother's mantle that betrayed her.

"What have we here?" a drunken voice yelled, so close that she leapt with fright and felt her heart pounding wildly. Then a hand grasped her roughly by one shoulder.

"I've caught me a little pigeon, boys," the voice shouted, slurring the words in a terrifying manner. "Let's have a look at her. Show a torch, Lepidus."

A torch came bobbing toward them from one direction and another torch flared as someone else ran up.

"Let's see her," Lepidus laughed.

Ruth tried to twist free. She was sobbing with terror.

Then the other man arrived. He held his torch high and looked at the other two.

The first man, whose meaty fingers had been digging into her shoulder, jerked his hand away and stepped backward.

"Good evening, captain," he said hurriedly. "We saw this girl skulking about. Thought she might be up to no good. We were going to bring her straight to you."

"I'm sure you were," the tall man said, his voice biting. "Get back to your posts and carry out your orders."

As they lumbered off, Ruth tried to make her legs race away but they were shaking so hard they wouldn't obey her. The man spoke to her kindly.

"What are you doing out alone?" he started to say. Then he swung the torch closer. "You're only a child," he exclaimed.

"Y-yes," Ruth got out through stiff lips. "I have to go to my grandmother. She's looking after a woman who's having a baby in the cow byre behind the inn."

He did not answer. He was staring at her in the light of the flare. When he finally spoke, his voice sounded strange, as though he had been running.

"Who are you?" he asked her. "Have you . . . have you a mother?"

"I'm Ruth," she said, growing calmer as she realized he meant her no harm. "My grandfather owns the carpentry shop here in Bethlehem and my grandmother is the village midwife. My mother died when I was a baby. I have to go back. Grandmother will miss me."

"I'll escort you," he said, his voice still strangely distant. "Tell me more about your family."

Ruth hesitated. She knew that her grandmother would not like her talking to a Roman soldier about private family matters. He WAS a Roman soldier, all right. She had figured out that much about him. But she had better answer. He had been kind. And it must sound odd, her talking only of her grandparents.

"My mother's name was Deborah," she said, her head down and her voice low. "She died. My father's family sent me to my grandparents when I was a month old. I think he is dead because he has never come to see me or sent a message. The man who brought me here said he had died. Susannah thought he was lying but she must have made a mistake."

Her voice had sunk to a whisper and he had to bend down to hear.

"Nobody will tell me about him. I don't even know his name," she finished.

"His name was . . . is Demetrius," the Roman soldier said quietly after a few seconds' pause.

Ruth took three more unsteady steps before her brain registered what her ears had heard. Then she stopped stockstill and stared up at the tall stranger. She could feel herself beginning to tremble again.

"Move along," called an irate voice. "How can I get my beasts past with the two of you blocking my road?"

The Roman captain scooped Ruth out of the way and apologized to the mule driver. Ruth had a moment to think over the astonishing thing the man had said. He must know her father. He must know her father well. Had he spoken to him of his daughter? No. Feeling muddled and frightened and wishing she were back with her grandmother, she waited.

There was lots of noise in the street but neither of them heard it. At last, she blurted out the question without giving herself time to become mute from fear.

"How do you know my father's name?"

The man hesitated.

"I was coming to see your grandparents tomorrow," he said instead of answering. "I'll be off duty in the afternoon. I should have come long ago. But when my mother told me that Deborah and the baby had died, I got myself posted to one of the colonies, thinking it might be easier to forget if I were far from where we had loved each other. I should have guessed. My poor mother was jealous of Deborah from the first. She could not bear people to know that my wife was a Jewish girl. She had the daughter of her closest friend picked out for me. If only I had asked more questions . . . Ruth, do you know what I am telling you?"

She did know but she could not believe it. This tall man her father! Why, she loved him already. He had kept her safe. And his shaking voice touched her. He would have come long ago if he had known where she was. Maybe, even though he had just found her, he already loved her too.

Such a startling thought was more than she could handle. She felt joyful but also a little confused and a little lost. She was astonished to find that she wanted to get away, to rush back to he strength and safety of her grandmother.

"I must go," she cired. "They need me to make the baby a bed. I have to hurry."

"You have your mother's eyes," he said. Then, big as she was, he swept her up into his strong right arm, carrying the torch held high in his left.

"Tell me where to take you," he ordered, his voice laughing but husky with tears too.

"In here," she said a few minutes later. "Are you coming in too? The baby . . . I don't think . . . Grandmother is busy."

"I will come to your house tomorrow, Ruth," he told her, setting her down at the low doorway. "I don't know what can be done. I have no home-place to take you to until this posting ends. But I will come. Are they kind to you?"

Ruth did not answer. She turned and ran inside, straight to the manger. Without looking to see what had happened in her absence, she pulled off her mother's mantle, doubled it and spread it carefully over the hay, smoothing it and tucking it in at the sides. You couldn't see the blue border now.

"Well done, Ruth," her grandmother said behind her. "Here he is, clean and swaddled and ready to sleep."

Ruth spun around and stared at the tiny new person with his small face topped with black downy hair cradled against her grandmother's shoulder. The woman stooped to lay him down when suddenly his face puckered and he began to wail piercingly.

"Oh dear. Well, you'll just have to cry then. Your mother needs me right now."

"Could I hold him?" Ruth asked shyly, reaching out her arms. "I can rock him and sing till he sleeps?"

"Good girl," her grandmother said again. Her eyes dwelt on Ruth's face as she gently transferred the baby from her arms to the child's.

"You do have such a look of . . . your mother," her grandmother said then.

The two of them stared at each other. Had Susannah, always so ready to take charge, kept them apart all these years? No, it was not Susannah's fault. They had let it happen themselves. Could the lonely time be over for both of them?

"He will give us a mantle of praise for a spirit of grief," Ruth's grandmother quoted under her breath.

Ruth began to walk up and down with the whimpering child.

"What's his name, Grandmother?" she called boldly, no longer needing to be only a silent shadow.

"Yeshua," his mother murmured.

Ruth began to sing.

> Your Abba shall hold you.
> Your Ema shall scold you.
> Your Safta shall rock you to sleep . . .

She would not tell them about her father's coming tonight, she thought. But how glad she was that she had found her grandmother before her father arrived. She had all the love one girl needed and more. Would her grandmother be kind to her tall new father? Yes, because he had loved her mother too. He still loved her. His voice had been filled with love. He would tell Ruth the things she so longed to know. Had her mother laughed a lot? Had she really been as brave as her grandmother thought?

"Yeshua," she whispered into the baby's tiny pink shell of an ear, "don't you be a mouse. Be a lion . . . a lion of love."

Then, seeing his mother was settled and at rest at last, Deborah's daughter carried the little boy over and placed him next to her as gently and deftly as her smiling grandmother could have done herself.

Ask ... Seek

Ask me "Did the angels sing?"
Ask me "Did his mother cry?"
Ask me "Did the shepherds kneel?"
Ask me "Why?"

I have no answers. I cannot
Say for certain what was real.
I only know that I have heard
That men did kneel.

I think his mother must have cried
—But turned from hurt to quiet joy
When she held within her arms
Her own small boy.

Ask me "Did the Magi come
Bringing gifts of myrrh and gold?"
I can but say that is the way
The tale is told.

Yet love has kept their story bright,
Love that started long ago.
It may have been in Bethlehem.
I do not know.

There was a man who lived this love.
Not the angels in the sky,
Not the shepherds, but this man . . .
Could he be "why"?

Within his love, there is a song;
And pain is there and crying too;
And humble men upon their knees;
That much is true.

But ask me "Is it relevant?"
And ask "What can it change today?"
Only those who seek . . . and kneel . . .
And love could say.

I'm a questioner like you,
Afraid to trust this answer "why."
Yet, tonight, if you'll come too,
I will try.

Let's walk inside the glowing myth.
They say he's there for all who go.
If I am brave enough to look,
This time I'll know.

We kneel—beside an empty crib.
You stretch a hand to me to share
My disappointment and, right then,
I see him there.

My Mother Got Me

My mother gave me a china doll
Like one she wanted when she was small.

I'd told her I wanted Dentist Barbie.

My mother gave me a string of pearls
Like her sisters got when they were girls.

I'd told her I wanted dangling earrings.

My mother gave me a music box.
To find it, she walked for blocks and blocks.

I'd told her I wanted the newest Spice Girls tape.

All I can say is
I'm glad I've got Grandma.
She has trouble hearing sometimes
But no trouble listening.

What Will the Robin Do Then?

Edward's fingers were numb with cold as he slid the last of his morning papers inside the Polosos' storm door and headed for home. Knowing tomorrow was Christmas Day and there would be no newspapers to deliver was a comfort, but it did not keep him warm.

He hugged himself, tucking his bare hands under his armpits. Then, with the empty canvas newspaper bag flapping against his leg, he stepped out briskly. Sometimes walking fast helped warm him up, but today, no matter how quickly he strode along, he went on feeling frozen to the bone. All he had to wear was a thin fall jacket.

Lois had told Harry his son needed a warmer coat.

"He's got a perfectly good windbreaker. He just likes whining," Harry had snapped, turning his back and banging out of the apartment.

But the "windbreaker" couldn't break this wind. Most kids quit wearing theirs before Hallowe'en. Edward didn't whine about it though. He might have if he had not known his father so well. Lois whined and got roared at and, sometimes, slapped.

Edward shivered. The early morning wind was from the north.

> The north wind doth blow
> And we shall have snow
> And what will the robin do then, poor thing?
> He'll sit in the barn
> And keep himself warm
> And hide his head under his wing, poor thing.

His mother's voice sang the rhyme. It was as though he had pressed a button on the TV. An image of her appeared, like magic, on the hazy screen of his memory and her soft voice, always tired but always loving too, recited the words about the wind and the robin.

He knew by now that it was dangerous to stare at her remembered face too hungrily or try to capture the exact tone of her voice. If he did, the vision would instantly dissolve and he would be left feeling the loss of her more keenly than before.

So he kept marching along, while he allowed himself to slip ever so gently back into his long-ago self.

He had wakened to see her standing by his window. They had lived in a small house then and he had had his own tiny room before Harry had lost his steady job at the stove company. Turning away from the window, his mother had caught him smiling drowsily at her. She had smiled back and recited the rhyme.

Then he had scrambled out of bed and run to join

116

her, wanting to see the robin. Instead, he had gazed out on a changed world, white with the first fall of snow. He could still feel his joy and astonishment and her arms holding him close. Had he been so small that he had forgotten what snow was? He was not sure. But he could not have been more than four because she had died the summer he turned five.

Another picture of her came before he could shut his mind against it. She lay, grey-faced, thin and silent, with closed eyes, in a high hospital bed. Harry's fingers had bitten into his shoulders, keeping him there, and Harry's voice screamed, as if it were still screaming now, "Damn you, don't leave us. If you won't stay for me, think of the boy. He needs you!"

Even when a nurse had come running and his father's shouting had turned to sobs, his mother's eyes had stayed closed. Edward had stared at her, waiting for some response, afraid of what it might be. But there had been nothing in her shut face to show she knew they were there. She had gone away before Harry shouted at her.

Edward wrenched his mind back to the present. There was nothing beautiful about this snow. It had fallen steadily for a week. Then, yesterday, it had half-melted, leaving the sidewalk slick with icy patches. His sneakers were soaked through and worn so smooth on the bottom that he kept sliding.

"Why don't robins freeze to death? They don't sit

around in barns here," he muttered, trying to forget his aching ears.

He knew the answer. No robins were left in Ontario. Birds could fly. Even the most birdbrained robin on earth would not choose to spend Christmas here. Edward would have gone weeks ago if he'd had wings.

He'd have to run or hypothermia would kill him. He'd seen a TV program on it and it was about to get him. He ran, jolting awkwardly from foot to foot. Just one more block to go!

Then their building came into view. It was not strung with coloured lights for Christmas but, when he saw a light come on in the rear window of their basement apartment, his heart lifted. That one lighted window meant Lois was waiting for him in the kitchen. The minute she heard him, she'd pour hot water into the big teapot so the two of them could have mugs of scalding hot tea. If there were enough bread, he'd have a peanut butter sandwich. He had eaten nothing before he left and the thought made his mouth water.

Crossing the paved parking area to the front door, he glanced at the ground-floor windows. No light showed there. The refugee family whom Lois had seen moving in yesterday must be sleeping.

Well, that figured. Harry had said many times that all the refugees swarming into Canada were lazy nogoods. Harry himself was rarely up before ten but Edward knew better than to mention it.

Eager for the warmth of a hot tea mug in his hands, .

Edward sprinted the last few steps, eased the outside door open, ran down the basement stairs as quietly as he could and slipped into the apartment like a thief. He did not want to wake either his father or Lois's little daughter Natalie.

Neither stirred. Harry's snores kept up their night music in the bedroom. Natalie, on her foam mattress in the corner, had lost her blanket but the cold had not yet wakened her. He had covered her up just before he went out. Now he leaned above her again and gently drew the fuzzy blanket back to her chin. Without opening her eyes, she snuggled into its warmth and smiled.

He smiled, too, and tiptoed on out to the kitchen.

"Welcome home, early bird," Lois said huskily, setting the kettle on the burner that worked.

She kept her back to him but he knew instantly that something was wrong. She was already dressed, for one thing. Usually she was only half-awake when he got back from his paper route. Her hair would be frowsy, her eyes gummed with sleep, her body wrapped in her grubby pink dressing gown. This morning, she had on street clothes and her hair was combed.

The joking words he had been about to say died on his lips. He stood still, staring at her back, waiting for her to face him. At last, with a sound that was half a laugh, half a groan, she swung around and Edward saw what his father had done to her.

Her right cheek was badly bruised and her top lip was split and swollen. He had heard them fighting last night but he had pulled his pillow over his head and willed himself into sleep to escape from the sound of Harry's rage and her weeping and pleading. He had not been able to hear most of the words but he had not needed to. It had happened every time Harry came home drunk and, lately, Harry had been drunk most of the time. That had been a big part of the trouble. Harry had had money to buy alcohol but not to get them enough food or decent clothes.

"Aww," he said, feeling sick at his stomach. "Why did you . . . ?"

He stopped himself. Lois had not deserved a beating whatever she did or said. He wished he had gone to help her even though, the times he had tried, it had made Harry madder and more dangerous.

"Don't look at me like that, Edward," she said. "I'm not permanently damaged. It looks worse than it is. Go take off that wet jacket and change into Harry's old slippers. I'll pour your tea."

Edward went. She was leaving. He knew the signs and he was sure he was right. It had happened before, after all. First there had been Francine. She had stuck around for almost two years. But after that, Crystal and Marianne had come one after the other and been gone in less than a month. Oh, and there had been that other one who had taken off after one weekend. He couldn't remember her name. He had not cared about any of them. He had been careful not to care. But Lois had seemed different.

Maybe Natalie made the difference. He had cared about her from the moment he laid eyes on her grinning face and big eyes.

The thought of her made him gulp. Maybe, just maybe, he was wrong. Maybe Lois was dressed because she was taking Natalie to the doctor and they'd be back tonight.

Natalie needs me, he thought. She must know Natalie needs me.

He knew it was not only that. He needed her too. As he turned to go back to where Lois waited, he remembered Harry shouting, "Damn you, Elsa, don't leave us. The boy needs you." Had his father felt the pain that Edward was feeling? If he had, why hadn't he been kind to Lois and stayed sober and found a job and . . . ?

I hate him, Edward thought bleakly. He's all the family I have and I hate him.

He forgot to take off his sodden jacket. Wearing the warm slippers, he went back to the kitchen, took the cup, gulped down one scalding mouthful of the dark brew and faced Lois.

"You're leaving, aren't you?" he demanded.

If there was any hope at all, he needed to know at once.

Lois, evading his eyes, grabbed the dishcloth and mopped the clean table top unnecessarily.

"I gotta, Edward," she mumbled, head bent, hand shaking.

"Harry's not so bad," he said weakly.

"I'm scared of him now and that's God's truth," she said. "What if he starts on Natalie?"

He stared at her.

"Hit her? You mean, hit Natalie? He wouldn't. Never," he said, stunned by her thinking such a thing, appalled at the possibility that she might be right. "Natalie's a little kid and she's . . . she's crippled. He wouldn't."

"He's hit you," she said simply.

He could not deny it. She saw her shot had gone home. She pulled out a chair and sat down next to him.

"It's not just Harry, Edward, honest," she hurried to explain. "I got a letter from my mum yesterday. You know how she said I was never to come home if I moved in with Harry. Well, now she says I can come home if I want because it's Christmas and we're family. So I've got a safe place to stay until I find a job."

Take me, he longed to say.

But he knew she couldn't. Besides, for some strange reason, he was stuck with Harry. He was all his father had left, too.

Except for Ronnie.

The thought of his half-brother made Edward's face stiffen with resentment. If Harry didn't have to give Francine money for child support, maybe he'd have enough left to take proper care of Lois and Natalie. Lois's pay cheque was barely enough to cover the rent and the phone bill. Lois had suggested doing without a phone, hoping to be rid of Francine's everlasting calls, but Harry had refused. He had to hear about his little pet and listen to the kid's mother saying he needed special shoes or whatever.

"I'd have stayed if it weren't for last night," Lois broke in upon Edward's thoughts. "You'd ducked off to bed before Harry came in with this big box from Sears. He'd gone and bought Little Lord Ronald a winter coat, a down-filled one, lined and everything, and I thought of you going out day after day in that rag he calls a "windbreaker" and I blew my top. I told him that it was high time he forgot Francine's spoiled brat and started paying attention to the great kid living right here in his house . . . That's when he began getting ugly."

Edward stared at her. If only . . .

"Don't look at me like that. I should have gone on and told him what I found out at work. You won't believe this, Edward," Lois said, pausing until she was sure she had his full attention.

"Won't believe what?" he said obediently.

"Tanya told me that slut of a Francine got married to some other guy six weeks ago. I couldn't help giving good old Harry the glad news last night. I oughta have known better. I thought he was going to kill me. It's a good thing he was too drunk to see straight."

"Married!"

Edward's yelp pleased Lois mightily even though she instantly shushed him.

"Right. Married. And still tormenting Harry."

She paused to check that the snores were still going strong, moved closer to Edward and lowered her voice to just above a whisper.

"What's more, Edward, there's something I didn't tell him. She's moving. This new guy of hers has a job out west and he's taking them along. They're leaving today."

"You mean . . . Ronnie . . . She's leaving and taking Ronnie."

"Of course. Can you picture dear Francine ditching her princeling? Get real, Edward."

Edward dropped his eyes. Her gloating expression turned her into somebody he did not know. And why was she so certain Francine would never abandon Ronnie? What did Ronnie have that he didn't? He had been ditched by everyone, hadn't he? Everyone but his father. Now even Lois was leaving him.

And she'd never leave Natalie behind.

If only she would! He took better care of the little girl than Lois did. He spent hours alone with her and took time to understand her garbled speech. He could look after her with no help from anybody. If only he were old enough to quit school . . .

Lois's voice cut through his thoughts as if nothing but her plans mattered.

"Edward, listen to me. I need your help. I gotta go to the diner and collect my pay and explain things to Tanya. I wish I could get Natalie a new coat. I hate taking her to my mum's in that old brown thing. But I'll have to. I got some stuff to pick up at Shopper's Drug. Can you take care of Natalie until I come back? Everything has to look normal until I pick her up or Harry will . . . Well, I don't know what he'll do. But I don't want to find out. Will you help me out, Edward?"

"Sure," he said automatically. "You go ahead."

She was leaving him to face Harry alone and all she could think about was making her escape. She was not worrying about what would happen to him later. Maybe she would forget he even existed once she and Natalie were safely away.

"You are a gem," she told him, her eyes swimming in tears again. "If you could have her outside the house, dressed to go, right at one, I'll come in a cab. My mother said she'd pay our way there and getting Nat down to the bus station any other way would be too hard. If Harry is around, take her up to the corner. But he won't be. I heard him tell Francine he'd be over there at one."

Edward nodded to show her he had heard and understood. As she rose, she caught sight of her bruised face in the mirror.

"My God!" she said and grabbed for her handbag. He watched her slather on make-up. She hid her bruise completely but could not disguise her split lip. She gave up, capped the lipstick and zipped the bag shut.

"I'd better get going," she said into the silence that lay between them. He heard the note of appeal in her husky voice but ignored it. She was deserting him. He would do as she asked but he was not about to comfort her by saying he and his father would get along fine on their own.

"If I don't get a chance to say Merry Christmas . . ." she started.

The look in his eyes stopped her. He could not bear to think about tomorrow. Well, there just wouldn't be any Christmas. He ought to be used to that, he supposed. They'd not had a real one since his mother died.

Lois shrugged into her coat, tied a scarf over her head and smiled crookedly at him.

Suddenly relenting, he did his best to smile back. Her face brightened instantly as though he had given her a present. Then she grabbed up her shoulder bag and hefted a bulging suitcase which had, until that moment, escaped his notice. She blew him a kiss and was gone.

He checked the clock. It was not quite eight yet. She'd go straight to the diner, he knew, to tell Tanya all about it. She wouldn't get out of there for a couple of hours. Then she'd do her errands.

Suddenly he realized he had not eaten and he was ravenous. He could not wait for the stale bread to toast. He slapped together a peanut butter sandwich and wolfed it down. He looked in the fridge for milk but there was only enough left for Natalie's cereal. He poured a second cup of lukewarm tea. Lois had not removed the tea bags and it was so strong it was black. He drained the cup anyway.

When he went in to Natalie, she was awake. She squeaked with delight at the sight of him. He put his finger to his lips and she tried to hush. But she found it almost impossible to be quiet when she was happy.

He dressed her in the clothes Lois had left on the chair. They weren't pretty, just an old jogging suit Lois had picked up at the Salvation Army store, socks that didn't quite match and her runners. She was very ticklish so she shrieked as he pulled the socks over her twisted feet.

"Hush up, Nat," he ordered but he was laughing himself.

Harry's snores checked but then went rasping on.

Edward propped Natalie up in the captain's chair and fixed her a bowl of Rice Krispies. As usual, she made him wait until they went snap, crackle, pop before she would eat. Even though she could only say a few garbled words, her joy was catching and, as he steadied her wildly waving spoon, he grinned.

When she was done, he wiped her mouth and parked her in front of the TV. He found cartoons but did not turn up the volume. Natalie didn't care whether she heard the sounds as long as she could watch the black-and-white picture. He settled down near her.

Harry got up at ten to ten. When he came out of the bedroom, Edward saw at once that he was in a foul temper. He clearly had a hangover. Natalie, who had been giggling at the antics of Bugs Bunny, was still.

"Where in the hell is Lois?" Harry growled.

"She's gone out," Edward said briefly, keeping his voice level.

"Out? Out where?"

Edward thought he heard fear in the shouted question.

"Shopping, I guess," he said, his gaze fixed on the picture tube. "She didn't say."

Harry spooned instant coffee into a big mug.

"When will she be back?" he asked, with his back turned.

"She didn't tell me. She just asked me to babysit until she comes."

Harry grunted. Then Natalie gave way to a shriek as Bugs Bunny toppled off a cliff. Harry turned on her.

"Shut up," he snarled. "Take her out of here, Edward. Kids need fresh air. My head's killing me. I can't stand her racket."

Edward did not argue. He wanted to get away before his father discovered that the suitcase was missing from the closet. He bundled Natalie into her mud-coloured mitts, her red scarf and her brown coat. It was not a coat meant for a little girl but for a tough kindergarten boy. It did nothing for Natalie. He wished, once again, that he could somehow manage to get her the kind of clothes worn by small girls in commercials.

Harry, seeing Natalie's eyes still fixed on the TV, lunged at the set and switched it off.

Edward set his teeth and pulled Natalie's hood up.

Then he got her out the door and half-slid, half-lugged her up the basement stairs. There the baby sled, especially built up for her, waited. Edward got her into it, tying her in. Then he opened the outside door.

It was pouring! Freezing rain. The sled would not go well in slush. But he did not want Harry to come blundering up and trip over them. And there was no way he would go back down and face his father's wrath.

There was the small entrance hall just inside the front door. They could shelter there temporarily. Once the icy needles of rain let up he might drag the sled to the library. They were always nice to him and Natalie in the Children's Room and Harry would never look for them there.

As he got the sled under the overhang outside the front door, Edward heard a car pull up. He turned to look. A big Volvo had drawn up to the curb. Edward, on the point of opening the door and getting the sled, with Natalie on it, inside, paused. Who on earth could it be?

The lady at the wheel opened her window a crack.

"Sonny, if you'll carry a box in there, I'll make it worth your while," she called to him.

Edward's heart leapt. If he had even one loony, he could take Natalie to Beckers and buy her some candy. He had handed over his paper route money to Lois so he had no cash. But if the lady wanted help . . . She might even give him a twoonie on such a miserable day.

"Hurry up, boy. I've got a lot to do this morning," the woman said sharply. "I'll pay you, I said."

Edward ran through the stinging rain to the waiting car. Glancing in, he saw that the lady was wearing a down coat and fleece-lined suede driving gloves. He tried not to show the anger that flamed up inside him.

"What do you want me to do?" he asked, shivering violently.

"Carry the cardboard box in the back to the ground-floor apartment. It's some winter clothes for the refugee family who moved in there a couple of days ago. It's not all that heavy. My husband carried it out for me."

Edward wondered if her husband was his size. He was skinny for ten and no Hercules. But he said nothing, just opened the rear door, hugged the large box to his chest and staggered toward the house. The lady sat and watched him.

"Poor Ed," Natalie mourned as he dropped the carton and turned to go for his money.

"Don't you worry, baby. I'm tough," he called softly.

But, when he reached the car, he had to stand in the stinging rain even longer because she had not yet fished her wallet out of her plump purse. He watched with avid eyes, seeing a thick wad of bills in the pocket she did not reach for. She dug through the coins in the zipped part and finally produced a dime.

"There you are," she said in a voice as sweet as syrup. "Oh, since it's Christmas, I'll make it a quarter."

He longed to throw the coin back at her but knew it would be silly.

"Wait now. I want you to give them a message. The clothes are from the U.C.W. at First Church," she told him. "Have you got that?"

"Yeah," Edward growled and turned to run. Before he could get away, she swept off, drenching his shoes and jeans with icy muck. Edward glared after her. But she did not glance back. She had given her orders.

He ran to where Natalie and the carton waited.

"Poor, poor Ed. So cold," the little girl mourned.

He grinned at her and hauled her into the little hall. Then he knocked on the door of Apt. 1A.

At first, there was not a sound. Edward was sure someone was there. He waited, listening hard. Nothing. Then a child began to whimper.

An older child, a girl, scolded the younger one in a foreign language. Footsteps approached the door.

"Who is?" the girl called, her voice shaking. She sounded scared.

"I have a box from the church for you," he called. "Winter clothes."

There was more silence. Then the door clicked open. A girl slightly smaller than Edward peered out with large dark eyes. She did not unhook the chain.

"Don't be scared," he told her. "Look."

Natalie waved her arms wildly and shouted, "Hi, hi."

Edward pulled up the cardboard flaps which hid the clothing from view. A man's raincoat, neatly folded, lay on top.

It looked about as warm as his thin jacket.

My windbreaker, he corrected himself.

But the girl seemed thrilled. She undid the chain and came out. A little boy followed, clinging to her skirt.

"Is your mother home?" Edward asked loudly.

"No. No madre," the girl answered him. After a moment, she added in a low voice, "Madre die. Soldiers shoot."

He could hardly hear her because the little boy was laughing at Natalie and returning her wild waves. Not knowing what to say about somebody's mother being killed like that, Edward pretended he had not caught her words. He shifted his attention to the boy now imitating Natalie.

"Hi, hi, hi," he was giggling, swinging his skinny arms around jerkily.

Edward's face froze. How dare this refugee brat make fun of her?

"Mario, vete," the girl snapped, yanking his arm down and pushing him back. Then she looked up at Edward.

"Entra. Come," she said, her eyes meeting his. "What is name?"

Edward accepted her unspoken apology. Mario was quiet but his eyes still smiled at Natalie. Maybe he just meant to be friendly.

"I'm Edward Fletcher," he said, "and this is Natalie."

The girl's face lit up.

"Eduardo," she said. "Natalia."

She clearly knew those names. She said them differently but they were recognizable. He looked at her more closely. She wasn't Indian, he was almost sure, and she didn't sound like the Vietnamese boys at school.

She beckoned them in and bent to drag the carton in after them. Edward hesitated but something in the apartment smelled wonderful. He undid the rope tying Natalie into the sled and got her onto her feet. Then he brought her in, holding her up as she jerked and jolted from one foot to the other. Mario stared at her until his sister told him not to in a string of unintelligible words.

No. The words weren't completely foreign. The girl had called him "estupido." Mario looked down and reddened. The girl turned to Edward.

"My name is Rosa," she said slowly and distinctly. Then she grinned and added, "Rosalita Maria Angelica Carmelita Lopez."

Edward could match that. For the first time in his life, he was proud of his whole name.

"Edward Morgan David Fletcher," he told her.

Rosa covered her mouth with her hand and giggled. Edward was pleased. The fear had gone from her eyes. Mario and Natalie seemed to be making friends too. He was patting her arm and saying "Hi" softly. Natalie chortled with delight and, trying to pat him back, swatted him on the ear.

"She can't help it," Edward hastened to explain. "She has cerebral palsy. She's smart but she can't walk or talk like other five-year-olds."

Rosa nodded as though she understood what he had said.

"In San Salvador," she said gravely, "Juanita same."

Edward, used to understanding Natalie, had no trouble following Rosa. San Salvador must be where she was from. Then he saw she was glancing sideways at the carton. He, too, wondered what else was in there. "Let's look," he said, kneeling next to the box.

Instantly she dropped down next to him and the two of them, with the younger children watching, unpacked the box.

There was a man's suit. It wasn't new or stylish but it looked pretty decent. There were two sweaters which might fit Rosa. They weren't pretty. One was greeny brown and thick. She pulled it on at once and looked grateful for its warmth. The other was pink but it felt prickly.

"Ahh!" Rosa exclaimed then.

She had spotted a thick, warm coat clearly meant for a girl her size. It was a lovely deep blue and it had a hood lined with scarlet. She snatched it up and thrust her arms into the sleeves. It was a perfect fit. She did up the belt and whirled around for them to admire its glory.

Edward's pleasure vanished when he saw that the coat had a stain near the hem in the back. He glared at it, anger boiling up in him. He did not want her to see but Mario pointed to it. Rosa twisted her body until she could see too. Her happiness clouded for a moment. Then she pleated the material swiftly with her fingers and the mark was hidden from sight.

"I fix," she told them. "I fix easy."

She laid the coat carefully over a chair and they went on looking. There were jeans, socks, underwear, a skirt and one dress. There were also two thick scarves, three pairs of handknit, striped wool mittens and, in the bottom of the box, a size 6 coat.

This time it was Mario who pulled it out and modelled it. Edward groaned. It was a girl's coat. It was pink with a wide skirt and pearl buttons. Pinned onto it were pink mittens and a pink toque. There was no other coat in the box. Mario was beaming at them, pleased as punch.

Rosa studied Edward's dismayed face.

"No good?" she asked.

Edward shook his head.

"It's a girl's coat," he said.

Rosa nodded. Her mouth thinned. Then she shrugged. She jerked the coat off of Mario and shoved it back into the empty box.

"Come," she commanded, looking from one to the other of them. "We eat, si?"

She did not wait for an answer but waved them to follow her to the kitchen. There, with a queenly gesture, she slid a casserole dish from the oven.

"A lady brings. Papa say we eat," she said.

Edward drank in the marvellous aroma of meat, tomatoes and onions. Dizzy with longing, he swallowed. The refugee kids were going to eat and Rosa must be asking him and Natalie to go home.

"We'll see you around," he said and bent to zip up Natalie's coat.

Rosa got there ahead of him. She took the coat off and put it on a chair. Then she set the table for four. They had been invited to stay.

Edward felt torn. He had never fed Natalie in front of strangers. Maybe she would be embarrassed. Harry would have a stroke if he knew they were eating refugees' food. But the stuff in the casserole smelled better than anything he had had for a long, long time. Lois had never cooked a meal with such mouth-watering smells.

"Eat, Edwa," Natalie said. "Natty eat. Eat, boy."

She was pointing at Mario. He backed away. Edward laughed.

"She just wants to stay," he explained, feeling shy, not knowing how to say "Yes" politely.

Rosa didn't wait for him to choose his words. She took one of Natalie's arms and motioned for Edward to grab the other. In no time flat, the four of them were sitting together around the kitchen table with Natalie in the captain's chair for support. Rosa had tucked a dishtowel under Natalie's chin for a bib and she, not Edward, was spooning the casserole deftly into Natalie's eager mouth.

"Mmmm," Natalie crooned between bites.

When they had finished the food, Edward knew it was almost time to get going. He got up to fetch their coats from the front room. Then, through the bow window, he saw his father starting up the street with a big box under his arm. Edward stepped back out of sight automatically but he looked on without much interest until he remembered, all at once, that in that box must be Ronnie's coat. If Harry was on his way, it must be almost one o'clock.

Lois would be here any minute to pick up Natalie. They had to hustle. There was no time to visit the library, no time to buy Nat some candy with his measly quarter.

It was as though the north wind had caught him again, chilling him to the bone. All the laughter and colour, the warmth and joy of the last hour, greyed into unreality. It was like the flickering picture the Fletchers got on their old black-and-white TV. The good time, the friendliness, even the wonderful food weren't really his. He shivered.

Clenching his fists to hold off the sick feeling for a few seconds longer, he turned and saw the others watching him with worried eyes. But how could he explain? He tried not to see the glow in Natalie's face dim as he fetched her brown jacket. If he had not had to put her coat on for her, he would have avoided looking at her.

The fabulous idea which rekindled his joy came to

him as he began poking her arm into the brown sleeve. Unlike his coat, hers was good and warm. And it was meant for a boy! With that knowledge came the vision of the pink coat lying hidden in the bottom of the carton. The other kids would tease the life out of Mario if he showed up at kindergarten in a pretty little girl's coat.

"Hey, Rosa, let's swap," he cried.

Rosa and Mario stared at his excited face without understanding until he pulled the brown coat off Natalie's arm, shoved it at Mario and, running to the box, hauled out the pink one.

"Si, si," Rosa cried, getting the idea at once.

She put Mario into the boy's coat while Edward bore the pretty pink clothes over to Natalie, who gazed at them in wonder. When he started dressing her in the lovely outfit, she began bouncing about with glee, shrieking and making Edward's job far harder. He didn't mind. He could hardly wait to see her dressed up as he had wanted to see her for weeks.

When he had her clothed in pink, he stepped back and looked.

"Wow!" he said softly.

"Wow, wow," Mario repeated, stroking his new coat. It wasn't nearly as nice as Natalie's but Edward knew from experience that Mario would be much happier looking like other boys. He would be different enough with his big black eyes and light brown skin and flood of Spanish.

I'll watch out for him, Edward thought.

He himself had no real friends but he could defend a little boy if things got tough. They'd be bound to go to his school.

Lois!

He dragged Natalie back into the hall and loaded her into the sled, tucking up the pink skirts. Then, waving goodbye to his new friends, he dragged her out to the street where he had agreed to be waiting for Lois.

Once they reached the curb, he stopped and fished out of his jeans the coin the church lady had given him. He put it carefully into Natalie's coat pocket.

"Merry Christmas, kid," he said, his voice gruff.

"Ma-ma!" Natalie cried, looking past him.

Edward swung around and saw Lois arriving in a taxi. She scrambled out and stared, round-eyed, at her small daughter.

"Wow, Ma-ma," Natalie shouted. "Wow! Wow!"

Edward did his best to explain but the taxi was waiting and Lois clearly could not take in all the details.

"I don't understand a word of it, Edward, but you are a living doll!" she cried. "When her grandma sees her, she'll love her. Oh . . . I wish we didn't have to go but we have to catch a bus. Goodbye, honey. God bless."

She was heaving Natalie into the cab as she talked. Edward, doing his best to help, did not let himself think.

"Get in," he told Lois. "I'll fasten her seatbelt."

He pulled it slowly out so it wouldn't snag and snapped it into the buckle. Then he grinned at the little girl whose new knitted hat had come down almost over her eyes.

"Be good," he said and adjusted it.

"Kiss," Natalie said.

He leaned forward and kissed her quickly. Her wet kiss slid across his cheek as her body jerked.

"You come?" she said, her eyes widening as he backed up.

He swallowed down a lump in his throat. Lois might not want him but Natalie did.

"Sorry, but I can't," he said, stepping up on the curb again as the driver turned on the ignition.

"I'll write, Edward. Honest!" Lois called, waving frantically.

He waved back, laughing. It was not a real laugh. Lois hated writing. She wouldn't even make a grocery list. He turned his back as the taxi pulled away. The cold he had felt earlier returned, gripping his heart and squeezing it bloodless. It was worse than anything the north wind could do to him. This cold would stay inside him forever.

Then he saw, with a shock, that the street was not empty after all. Harry, the big box still under his arm, was running down the hill toward him, shouting something.

Edward braced himself and waited.

"Where did she go?" Harry yelled again, skidding to a stop right next to Edward. "Where?"

"Who?" Edward said, playing for time, struggling to think what he should say.

"You know who! Lois. I saw her in that taxi and she had the kid with her. Why didn't she leave her with you? Where's she gone?"

"I don't know," Edward lied.

Harry's big hand swung back as though he was going to strike his son. The box slid, almost falling to the snow. Harry grabbed it and brought his heavy hand down on Edward's shoulder and shook him.

"When did she say she'd be back? I'll make her pay ... She'll be back with her tail between her legs ..."

"No," Edward said, too tired suddenly to go on lying. "Not this time. She's taken her stuff. She's left."

Harry stood there, looking as though he had been punched out. Still hanging onto Edward's shoulder, he swayed. Then he slid his hand down to his son's upper arm.

"Your coat's wet," he said in a strange thick voice. "When you go in, take it off, Edward. You mustn't get sick."

Edward blinked. He felt confused. What had come over his father?

Harry Fletcher turned without another word and stumped off down the street.

"When will you be back?" Edward called after him.

But his voice was thin and weak and the wind, whining through the tree branches, drowned out his question.

He went into the empty apartment. As he pulled off his sodden jacket, something fell out of one of the pockets. He bent to get it, certain it was nothing of his. He found one pair of handknit striped mittens, rolled into a neat ball.

It took him a full minute to recognize them. They were the large mitts which Rosa had tried on her small hands. They had been way too large for her and Mario had giggled as she made them flap up and down. She must have put them in his pocket while he was getting Natalie into her sled. His heart stirred slightly. But too much was hurting for him to realize he had just received a Christmas present. Putting the mitts down carefully, he draped his soaking jacket over a chairback. Then he picked up Natalie's fuzzy blanket, wound it around his shivering body, grabbed up the mittens and sank down on the sagging couch.

He stared at the TV. It was turned off but he looked at it anyway, seeing not his mother or even Lois but his father walking away from him. A full five minutes crawled by before he noticed the screen was blank. Another five went by before he got up and switched the television on.

He watched one commercial after another. Santa chuckled and boomed "Ho, ho, ho!" at him while trying to convince him that he wanted the newest cereal, the newest video, the latest toy. Edward barely noticed. He'll have to come back, he whispered. He has nowhere else to go and nobody else to go to.

He refused to think about what he would do if Christmas came and Harry was still missing.

Finally he grew hungry enough to get himself another peanut butter sandwich. Then, after watching two Christmas specials, he fell into an exhausted sleep.

It was dark when he woke. Nobody was there. Yet he had heard something. Could it be Lois? Had she thought of his being there all alone and come back?

Then he saw it was not Lois who had come in but Harry.

"You're back!" Edward said, his voice shaking with relief.

Harry didn't speak. He came across the room, stumbling over the rug.

Not really drunk, Edward thought. Only a little.

Then Harry dropped something. The coat box from Sears. And he was standing there, just standing, grinning down at Edward.

What's he scared of? Edward thought.

Then he saw that Harry was holding up a coat. It was a brand new coat, with a down filling and a fleece collar. It had pockets and there was a hood zipped in at the back. Edward knew Francine had been gone when his father reached the townhouse where she lived. Harry must have returned the small coat and exchanged it for this one. It was not for Ronnie. Instead it was exactly the right size for a skinny, ten-year-old boy.

Worn out by the long day but somehow feeling deep

inside himself a flicker of hope, Edward reached out and pulled the coat toward him. His father, holding tight to it, came too. He landed on the couch with a thud and stayed there, breathing heavily, looking hungrily into his son's face. Then, at last, Edward leaned his head against his father's warm bulk and the wonderful coat and cried.

And this time, Harry didn't yell at him to "Quit it!" This time, as he gathered up his son, Harry was crying too.

Plenty

I have plenty of everything but want.
I try to imagine hunger,
Try to believe I have not eaten today,
That I must stand in line for a bowl of soup,
That my cheekbones angle out of my hollowed face;
But I smell the roast in the oven.
I hear the laden refrigerator hum.

I think of people whose walls are made of wind.
I stand outside in the cold.
I tell myself I am homeless and dressed in rags;
But my shiver lacks conviction.
I stand in fleece-lined boots and a winter coat.
Home is a block away.

I leave my wallet at home.
Pretending I have no money,
I walk past stores and wish.

"I have no money, no money at all, no money."
I turn my head in shame as I pass the bank.

I pay for a parcel of food. I gather clothes.
I adopt a child through a foster parent plan.
I do what I can. I am generous. I am kind.
I still have plenty of everything but want.

January

Roads

Some people walk on straight roads
And see to both ends
—But my road dips and loops and swoops
And crooks and bends.

I've heard some people tell the world
That they know where they're going
But that's a thing I couldn't stand:
Always knowing!

Charlotte's Celebration

When Charlotte Cooper and most of her Grade Five class graduated from Walnut Grove Elementary and started attending Grade Six at Queen Elizabeth Senior School, Charlotte liked it just fine— until December. She was in Mr. Broome's class, for one thing. He was the first homeroom teacher she had had who was a man. When she made a joke and he got it, his deep laughter startled and pleased her.

But December came, of course. They had a student teacher by then and Charlotte hoped having Ms. Mendoza there might change the holiday unit which always hit in December. Maybe, for once, nobody would make a big deal out of Christmas and Hanukkah and Diwali. Mr. Broome, who sang bass in two choirs, loved the sound of his own voice. He might just keep talking and never require class participation. That would be wonderful.

But on December 1st, he dashed her hopes.

"Today, class, we are beginning a new unit," he said. "We're going to study how different cultures celebrate midwinter festivals."

Charlotte glowered at his rosy face and longed to walk out.

"Are you okay, Charlotte?" Tanya Zabrinski asked in a whisper. "You look like you bit into a sour pickle."

"I'm fine," Charlotte whispered back.

Tanya returned her attention to Mr. Broome. She loved the holiday unit. It was full of stories and songs and food and during it, math was often forgotten. Everybody but Charlotte was pleased. She might have liked it too if teacher after teacher had not insisted on everyone telling how he or she celebrated at home. Maybe Mr. Broome would skip that part?

Mr. Broome had a lot of rehearsals to attend. Getting his students to fill up class time talking about family traditions allowed him to skip hours of lesson planning. He could just nod at their stories and then send them to the school library to research St. Nicholas or where the first yule log came from.

"Now I want each of you to describe to the rest of us how your family will be observing this holiday," Charlotte heard him say. "With so many different backgrounds, we should learn lots. We want to hear about gifts, songs, special foods, whatever you do to mark the holiday season. Tanya, let's start with you."

Tanya jumped up eagerly and launched into a list of Christmas customs her family had brought with them from Poland.

"Wonderful, Tanya," Mr. Broome said. He looked

over their heads at Ms. Mendoza, who was sitting observing at the back.

Charlotte glanced back at her too.

Ms. Mendoza looked totally unlike every other student teacher they had had. Her hair was black as soot and hung straight down her back in a thick braid. Her eyes were a deep brown and, when she laughed, they narrowed into gleaming slits. They always seemed filled with secret joy. Now she stared coolly back at Mr. Broome as though she was bored by him but trying not to let it show.

"How about you, Norman?" Mr. Broome said, turning away.

One by one, the kids stood up and spouted off something they did during the holidays. They had family dinners. They went carol singing. They decorated Christmas trees. They lit Hanukkah candles. On and on and on . . .

Charlotte suspected that some of them never darkened the door of a church or temple or synagogue. But they still had turkey for dinner or latkes for supper, presents under the tree or at their grandmother's, specials to watch on TV or special clothes to wear.

They all have something to sing about, she thought bleakly. Everybody but me.

Maybe she could lie. Mr. Broome would not know that her family did nothing. She could say that Santa brought gifts and they decorated a tree and leave it at that. Nobody would tell. They might not even remember. Maybe it was only a big deal to her.

But why should she have to lie?

She wasn't ashamed of her family. Mum and the older boys were okay and she loved Dad and Michael with her whole heart. She and her mother had struggled for years to change each other, but lately they had given up the battle and were getting along better. Charlotte was the eldest and she had had to mind the boys a lot so they resented her. But they knew they could not manage without her. She packed their lunches, did a lot of their laundry, bullied them into going to bed more or less on time and kept the Cooper household on track—almost.

"You're better with those hoodlums than I am," Mum had said not long ago. "I'm always having to threaten to tell their father on them."

In her slapdash, hurried way, Mum loved them all but the older boys were her favourites. Dad cared about Charlotte more deeply, she suspected, although he tried not to show it. He was a quiet man who did not hug kids or smile at them a lot. All four children trusted him completely.

Just the same, Charlotte rarely took friends home with her and, when she did, she rushed them out the door as soon as she could manage it. The house was such a mess, the boys were so loud and grubby and Mum too eager to tell them her troubles.

Until January, nobody in Mr. Broome's sixth grade

class was putting a foot inside the Coopers' front door, if Charlotte had anything to say about it . . .

"Charlotte, tell us how your family celebrates," Mr. Broome said.

Charlotte did not give herself time to be tempted.

"We don't," she said baldly, not lowering her voice or trying to soften the abrupt words.

"What do you mean?" the teacher said, taken aback for once.

"We don't celebrate. No mince pies, no potato pancakes, no dreidls, no stockings hung by the chimney with care, not at my house."

"But, Charlotte, there must be . . ."

"No, Mr. Broome, there is nothing. We don't believe in any of it so we don't pretend."

Mr. Broome stopped smiling. He stared at Charlotte through narrowed eyes. She guessed that he thought she was making the whole thing up.

The other kids had begun whispering to each other and shifting in their seats. Ms. Mendoza cleared her throat as though to speak. But, just then, the man's face brightened.

"I apologize, Charlotte. Nobody told me you were Jehovah's Wit . . ."

"We aren't Jehovah's Witnesses," Charlotte cut in. "We're not Communists either. And we don't belong to some stupid cult. We're just disbelievers. My father says life is simpler if you believe in nothing."

Mr. Broome was embarrassed now. He was angry,

too, although, Charlotte figured, he was mad at Mum and Dad, not Charlotte herself. He looked around the room, stalling, trying to decide what to do next. His cheeks were beet red and his expression was just like her brother Morgan's when he was sulking.

Charlotte knew her own cheeks were flushed. She set her chin. Perhaps anger flashed in her eyes also. Why didn't he just move on?

"Well, it doesn't matter, of course," the teacher said finally. "I just never thought . . . But let's move along. How about your family, Susan?"

Everybody, Charlotte included, heaved a sigh of relief when Susan began a long story about her father's taking them to some farm to cut down their own tree. They had done it every year she could remember. Mr. Broome smiled. This was exactly what he wanted, family traditions.

Charlotte's bad moment had passed. Now the loneliness would set in. She turned in her seat so the light from the window would not show her face so clearly and caught the student teacher looking at her.

Ms. Mendoza rose quietly and came up to Charlotte's desk. She was smiling faintly. Under the cover of Dan's telling about Japanese New Year, she said softly, "I wonder if you realize how lucky you are."

Lucky? Charlotte kept silent, waiting.

"You don't have to do all over again things your family has done every Christmas for years. You can invent a celebration all your own. You can make up the stories, create the special food, even find the songs . . ."

Charlotte glared at a crack in her desk lid and growled, "I don't celebrate. That's it. I don't need to celebrate."

"I think you'll discover that celebration is like eating and singing. You can't live a rich life without doing it."

"What do you celebrate?" Charlotte demanded, her voice angry.

"I have something very special to rejoice about this year," Ms. Mendoza said.

Then, before Charlotte could ask any more questions, the bell rang and it was time for lunch. After that morning, Mr. Broome just read the class stories and taught them songs without trying to include every child's personal faith. Charlotte loved the stories.

Even though none of them reflected her family's customs, they all belonged to her in some deeper way. When they read *The Best Christmas Pageant Ever*, some of the kids sent her sideways glances as though they thought her family must be like the Herdmans. They weren't. The Coopers knew the Christmas stories as well as anyone. It was hard to believe that kids could be as ignorant as Imogene and her brothers and sister. Even so, Charlotte laughed at the funny parts and felt a lump come into her throat when the poor family gave the ham from their Christmas hamper to the baby Jesus.

Her autumn friendships with Tanya and Elizabeth cooled. They were busy shopping and hanging around their homes and going to parties and concerts. At last, the Christmas vacation came.

Then Charlotte hung around her own house, helping, helping, helping. She was tidy and Mum wasn't so she had lots to do. She cleaned the fridge out first. It was a disgusting job but worth it in the end. Then she started washing, drying and putting away clothes. There were hundreds of wandering socks to track down and match up. There was plenty to keep her busy.

Matthew was five. Morgan was nearly four and Michael, the baby and her secret favourite, was almost two. On Boxing Day, their father gave each of them a book.

"They're my Un-Christmas presents to you," he said gruffly.

Charlotte remembered the "unbirthday presents" in *Alice's Adventures in Wonderland* and grinned. She read Michael *Goodnight, Moon!* many times before she escaped with her book, *The Moor Child*. The cover had a picture of a strange little girl playing bagpipes. Charlotte loved it. Dad said he had read it. Did he suspect that she thought she might be a changeling?

Then it was January. School and Guides began again.

A mystery was solved when Tanya announced at Guides that her mother had met Ms. Mendoza somewhere and learned that the teacher was pregnant.

"Oh," Charlotte said softly, understanding why the teacher's eyes had looked so joyous.

Charlotte walked most of the way home with Tanya. Mum, who went around in terror of kidnappers, serial killers and motorcycle gangs, thought she was safe enough walking the last two blocks on her own.

"Just step lively and come straight home," she said.

Charlotte walked briskly but she did not hurry. She looked forward to the two-block walk. It was almost the only time she was alone in the whole week. Her brothers seemed to fill every centimetre of the little house. She shared her room with Michael. Before his birth, the room had belonged to her alone and she had loved reading before she fell asleep. But she loved Michael too with his curls and his merry grin and his way of charging to hug her the minute she came in from school.

Thank goodness Christmas was over, she thought, glancing at the darkened church across the road. Their new chimes had stopped relentlessly playing carols. The same four carols over and over again.

"'Silent Night,' my foot! To think I used to like Christmas music," Dad had snarled one night and slammed out of the house.

At school, the January review had started in earnest. As usual, math had been neglected in December and they had to do hours of it to make up. Charlotte didn't mind. There was nothing personal about math.

She slowed down. It was a glorious night. There was no moon. But the stars shone like a million . . . stars.

Suddenly she thought of the student teacher's quiet words. "I think you'll find celebration is like eating and singing. You can't live a rich life without doing it."

"Stars!" Charlotte Cooper cried, laughing aloud. "I'll celebrate the stars. That way, I can have a holiday every clear night. I won't have to keep to one date."

She thought of star-shaped cookies, "Twinkle, Twinkle, Little Star," the constellations. She could have a Big Dipper Day. And toast the Milky Way with a vanilla milkshake.

The possibilities were endless.

It was too cold to stand around though. She went inside. The boys were all in bed and Dad and Mum were watching TV. Charlotte opened the door, waved at them, and went upstairs.

She crept into the crowded room she and the baby shared, but the moment she eased open the door, she heard Michael stirring. By the time she was inside and had put her Girl Guide stuff down, he was standing up in his crib and saying, "Up, Lott. Up," in a sleepy little voice.

She went over and lifted him out of the crib. He snuggled against her, putting his face into her neck and cheeping like a baby bird. She sat down in the rocking chair and gave him a drink of water. Then, when he was almost asleep, she rose to put him back in his bed.

"Michael," she whispered suddenly, "Michael, would you like to see stars?"

He was too sleepy, she knew, but she carried him over to the window and pulled back the curtain.

"Look!" she said, turning her body so he was facing out. "Look, Michael. See the stars."

He raised his head but he was looking at her. He reached up and grabbed a fistful of her hair, gave it a friendly tug and then put his head back on her shoulder.

"Night-night, moon," he murmured, yawning hugely and shutting his eyes tight.

Charlotte laughed.

"All right. We'll let the moon in too," she said. "I'll show you the stars when you're wider awake. You know what? You and I are going to celebrate the night lights."

Joy surged up in her and she laughed softly. She felt as though she were being pulled into a throng of dancers. The earth had turned toward light again. With the darkness and loneliness of December behind and a year filled with starlight ahead, she was ready to celebrate at last. And as she gazed up, one last time, the sky flashed down, especially for her, Charlotte Cooper, light as beautiful as the candles on a menorah, as enchanting as those strung through Christmas tree boughs, as radiant as the torches carried in every festival around the world.

I Resent the Tidy People

I resent the tidy people
With their worthy ways,
Rising promptly to get started
On their useful days.

Early birds and high achievers,
Shoulders to the wheel,
Never aimless, never idle,
Doing work that's REAL.

Making New Year's Resolutions,
Keeping every one,
None of them nonsensical,
Frivolous or fun.

They're so sensible, so knowing,
Efficient, brisk, mature.
"No one's perfect"—but it's plain
That they're superior.

They schedule time and budget money.
They carry projects through.
I like to wake up in the morning
And wonder what I'll do.

I'm surrounded by the creatures.
They set things straight. They cook.
They organize and check off lists
While I sit with a book.

I sit and read. I dream. I doodle.
I drowse. I write a rhyme.
I'm FREE—so why do I feel guilty
Over half the time?

I suppose it's partly envy.
Idlers, like me,
Are out of place within their hive
Of endless industry.

Sometimes I have this awful urge
To show them—but how dull
If I, in turn, should grow to feel
Indispensable.

What bliss, though, to belong, to be
One of the throng that strives
To own a dust-free universe,
To lead essential lives!

Oh, to be so bright and busy,
Inwardly so made
That you've no time to be haphazard,
Lonely or afraid . . .

Yet when do they find hours for dreaming?
When get poems done?
I resent the tidy people.
Thank God I'm not one!

If I Wait

If I wait,
Spring will come.
Buds will break.
Bees will hum.

Flowers will bloom.
Birds will sing.
If I wait,
It will be spring.

This my song
As out I go
To face a century
Of snow.

City Boys

When Mum told us the news, we thought she must have gone stark, raving mad. What else could we think when without warning, out of the blue, she announced she was taking our whole known world and standing it on its head?

We were used to her being impulsive. We did our best to protect her from her goofy ideas. For one moment, both of us hoped that this was another of those whims and we could talk her around without much trouble. Then we looked at her and all hope perished. She would not look so uptight over a whim.

"You'll love the country," she assured us, her voice high, her eyes begging us to be enthusiastic. "And you know you both already like Will."

"Will's okay," I said into the silence. "I like him. But he's not our father. He doesn't feel like a father to me."

"Me neither. Why can't you marry him and live on this farm of his?" Daniel put in, fighting to sound grown-up, fighting not to yell at her, fighting not to panic. "And we can visit you on weekends and during vacation. Lots of guys at school do that. It's not that I don't like Will but let's face it, Mum. David and I are city boys."

I was astounded at my younger brother's brilliance. I mean, we'd had less than five minutes to think. For a few seconds, as she stared down at the carpet, I thought she might even be considering what Daniel had said. Then she raised her head and looked at us squarely and we both knew things were not going to be that simple.

Daniel sighed. If I didn't sigh too, I felt like it. Then we waited for the bad news which was written all over her face.

"First of all, once I marry Will, your father's family won't pay your school fees any longer. I don't blame them. Thomas left not only lots of debts for them to settle but a wife and two sons who needed their help. They've been very kind to us. But it isn't only the fees. I want you with me. If you can't bear the idea of my marrying Will, I'll tell him I'm sorry but you boys come first."

She petered out then. But both of us heard the change in her voice. It was like a bright, helium-filled balloon one minute and a limp bit of latex the next. All the joy had gone. She was blinking back tears and struggling not to let us see.

We couldn't let her make a big sacrifice for us. She'd already made plenty. We knew, although she did not guess that we'd been told, that my father's brother had offered to adopt us when Dad died. He has plenty of money and a nice big house in Ottawa. She could have visited us whenever she liked and lived much more comfortably than she did with us to support. Apparently she never even thought it over.

"My boys and I are a family," she said. "I couldn't let them go."

Our cousin Ralph told us. He'd heard his parents telling my other uncle and aunt. They had all agreed she was out of her skull. Ralph was making fun of her when he told us, but we did not laugh.

"It'll be great really," Daniel said suddenly. "We can . . . we can go to the Royal Winter Fair with Will and win prizes for our cows."

I snorted. What a dope! But he was trying. I talked fast, struggling to sound more convincing than my brother. After all, I am nearly eleven months older and so have more maturity. That's what I tell him anyway.

"When's the wedding?" I asked. "Do you want us to be ring bearers?"

She burst out laughing at that and her face lit up again. She was not completely fooled but she was comforted. And she was relieved. Very, very relieved.

"I told Will that my boys are the best in the world," she said proudly. "He thinks I spoil you. But he'll soon see for himself what great kids you are. And it won't be hard for you to adjust. After all, you're still young."

At that moment, we were both ten. My eleventh birthday came two weeks later.

The two of us winced but she did not notice. We waited for her to busy herself in the kitchen so that we could talk without having to choose our words so carefully. But, when this happened, we just sat and looked at each other for a long time.

"We're city boys," I muttered finally. "Will won't like having us around."

"Do you suppose we'll have to get up when some dumb rooster crows and do the milking before we set out for school?" Daniel asked.

He was doing his best to sound rough and tough but I could hear the quiver in his voice. We always know that sort of thing about each other without needing to talk about it. It comes from being almost twins maybe and from being fatherless so early and from having had to change countries.

"It's probably a one-room schoolhouse and we'll have to walk five miles to get there," I said.

Daniel grinned. It wasn't the best grin I've ever seen on his face but it cheered me up a bit.

Neither of us mentioned what we were really worried about. Our father, Thomas Ling, had been Chinese. Mum was black. We were very brown with curly hair and black eyes. If the kids in our new school looked like Will, they'd be white with corn-yellow hair and eyes as blue as the country sky. At our private school in Toronto, there were lots of kids who weren't white. We had stood out even there, not because of our mixed race, but because everyone knew our dad's family paid our way and our mother worked in an office. At first, we had English accents like the kids in our school in Nigeria, but we shed those as fast as possible. We were a team. Anybody picking on either of us had to fight both of us. So we were left alone.

Mum dropped her bombshell at the beginning of October. We were to finish out the term and then, at Christmas, they would be married and we'd move to Will's farm. We'd start attending the new school in January.

"I think you'll like the school," Will said when he picked us up the following weekend. "My nephews went there and my niece Hilary is there now. She lives right across the road from our place. She's your age so she can show you around."

"That should be hilarious," Daniel said under his breath.

Will did not answer. I hoped he had not heard. If Daniel comes up with a smart remark, he doesn't think. He just blurts it out.

We visited the farm a couple of times before December. Will had cleared out a big attic room for us. I have to admit it was the greatest place we've ever been given. We'd always had a tiny room with bunk beds in the small apartments where we lived. Just room enough for the two of us and S.P., our African pygmy hedgehog. S.P. stands for Stickly Prickly, the hedgehog in the *Just So Stories*. She lives in a thirty-gallon aquarium and she sometimes seems to take up more room than we do even if she is not much bigger than my two fists put together when she curls up in a ball.

Our old room was cramped but we were at school most of the time. On Saturdays, we almost always went out on expeditions. The Ontario Science Centre was Daniel's favourite place to hang around and the Royal Ontario Museum was mine. I'm fascinated by old stuff—dinosaurs, Egyptian mummies, of course, but other stuff too. Old coins and weapons and maps and books. We both enjoyed going to the SkyDome to see the Jays play when Mum had the money, and we liked the library near our place. Then there was the video arcade, although Mum hardly ever let us go there.

"I wonder what you do on Saturdays in the country," Daniel said one day, as we stared at the dinosaur skeletons in the ROM.

"Bird watching," I said. "Hikes. Um . . ."

My brother shuddered.

"Never mind," he said. "I don't want to know."

We stayed with school friends until the newly married couple came back from their honeymoon. They went to Arizona for a week. Daniel said that if they took us along, we'd stay in the hotel swimming pool and not bother them one bit. But Will just laughed.

We all, S.P. included, moved to Will's place, which we were supposed to think of as "home," on New Year's Day and we arrived in the middle of a blizzard. The old stone farmhouse loomed up like something in a horror movie. We fought our way through a howling wind and driving snow and fell through the front door.

"Welcome to Hurricane Hall," said a too sweet voice.

"This is Hilary," Will said. "Hilary, this one is Daniel and this other one is David."

Hilary was a skinny girl with hair so fair it was nearly white. Her blue eyes were sharp and not friendly. Hostile even. She made them go wide.

"Ohh," she breathed. "I thought they were invaders from a new galaxy."

We must have looked startled, for Will laughed.

"Don't start teasing them yet, Hilary," he said. "Remember, they're city boys."

Neither of us liked that. But I suppose it was just as well to get started hearing it. We were to hear it over and over again during those first difficult weeks. Even S.P. was a handicap. Country boys don't have pet hedgehogs. Hilary, our trusty little guide, made sure that everybody knew about her.

"You know what, David? I think she's jealous," Daniel murmured into my ear, after watching our stepcousin gazing at S.P. sleeping in her nest of rags and broken branches.

I, too, had finally figured that out. Cows are fine, in their place, but their place is in the barn. All Hilary's animals were there for practical purposes. Even the dog was a working collie who seemed not to notice anyone but Hilary's father. The cats were barn cats and not at all tame. And the cows were not cosy animals for all their fancy, girlish names.

What Daniel had not yet figured out was that Hilary was jealous of us too. It had only dawned on me a few hours earlier when Will had taught Daniel how to milk a cow by hand instead of by machine. Daniel had mastered milking in no time flat while I could only get a drop or two and highly irritated Rosabelle while I was at it. Will grinned down at my brother and told him he'd make a farmer yet. And I, glancing up, saw the raging jealousy in Hilary's eyes as she watched. It was then I understood why she was as mean as a snapping turtle in all her dealings with us. Will was all hers before we arrived.

Her parents were serious-minded people who seemed to think of nothing but work, talk of nothing but work and do nothing but work. Hilary was the wrong sex and the wrong size to be their child. She was so skinny she looked as though she were made of pipe cleaners. Uncle Will, though, thought she was special and gave her the loving attention she lacked at home. She was the only child in his life before we city boys arrived.

I did not think this all out in words the moment I saw why she hated us, but I have put it together since. Mum and I have talked it over and she agrees that Hilary has had a rough deal. Mum gave Hilary so much of her time that Daniel and I were beginning to resent her, too, until I got it straight. Mum never had a daughter. That's part of the picture.

A month later, however, Hilary was so busy talking about some lost dog that she hardly saw us.

"Whose dog is it?" I asked.

She answered me in a straightforward voice, worried but not unfriendly. The minister of the little church not far from Will's house was found dead. It was his dog that had vanished. We had seen the minister at the church a few times but I had not known he had a dog. Daniel had not heard of her either. But we had liked the man and we were sorry. In my mind, I pictured a lost spaniel or perhaps a border collie. A lot of farmers around our part of the world seemed to go for them. I figured she had probably turned up at somebody's back door and I was grateful to her for distracting Hilary from her war against us. I had no idea this particular dog was going to loom large in our lives.

I had forgotten her completely when Hilary's parents decided to go with Mum and Will to a church "story fest" in Toronto. They were going to get a babysitter and Hilary was to stay over at our place so one babysitter would be all that was needed. I thought Daniel and I were old enough to be left on our own but my mother told me Hilary's parents would not hear of such a thing.

"Besides," she said, "you three may require a referee."

"Ha, ha! Very funny," I said but I could see she might be right.

The sitter had not arrived when it was time for the grown-ups to leave and Hilary's parents got into a real tizzy. Mum phoned and learned that Faith Turnbull had already left to come to take care of us.

"She'll be here in twenty minutes," she said, hanging up.

"Go ahead and leave," I told her. "We can look after ourselves for twenty minutes. We can sit and watch TV until she gets here. We'll be safe as houses."

"We'll be what?" Hilary asked.

"Safe as houses," I repeated. "It is an urban expression. Go on, Mum. You'll miss the beginning if you don't."

Mum and Will had met at one of these story nights. They are both big on church. Anyway, when Daniel and Hilary agreed that we'd stay sitting there for the whole twenty minutes, the grown-ups piled into Will's van, waved and took off.

And we did sit there for twenty minutes. We sat there for twenty-five, thirty, forty minutes. Just as we were getting nasty to each other because we were worried, the phone rang. It was the hospital. Faith had been in an accident and would not be able to come.

"We'll put her on the line," the nurse said. "She's very upset. Don't keep her talking any longer than you can help."

Faith sounded hysterical at first. It turned out that she been hit by another car on her way over and she had not done up her seatbelt yet. So she had pitched forward and broken her nose, one wrist and a couple of ribs.

"I look as though I've been in a war," she wailed. "And they won't let me out of here until tomorrow. Even if they did, my car is a wreck and can't be driven.

David, can you manage? I feel so terrible about this. Your parents trusted me . . ."

The nurse removed the phone from her hand and asked if she should call Mum.

I told her not to worry.

"We'll be just fine," I promised.

"Don't say we'll sit in front of the TV," hissed Daniel.

I almost had done exactly that. The nurse took my word we'd be fine without asking how old we were or anything. She hung up and the three of us were on our own.

"Let's make popcorn," Daniel said.

That did it. He's a genius. Hilary loves popcorn. In three shakes of a skillet, the three of us had popped a huge pan of fluffy, white popcorn, drenched it in melted butter, salted it and gotten ourselves a big bowl each. We were sitting in front of the TV, contentedly munching and watching an old King Kong video, when we heard the knock on the front door.

It was not a regular knock. It was more like a scratching sound followed by a sort of thud. Even though I had never heard anything like it, I automatically got up to see who was out there.

"No! Stay here!" shrieked Hilary, the calm country girl. "It might be a vampire or . . . or a sex maniac."

I settled down again but I was not one bit relaxed. Every nerve in me was braced for the knock.

Scratch, thump!

Hilary's eyes were like saucers and Daniel's hand, scooping up more popcorn, was trembling so violently that he was dropping more than he held onto. I could see it across the room. They were heading for hysterics.

Then we all heard another thump and a kind of howl.

I am the eldest. I have a little sense. Before I could go into a panic like theirs, I jumped up, ran to the big front door and swung it open.

Outside it was storming. I could not see the trees on the far side of the driveway for blowing snow. But I could see the monstrous shaggy creature who had been knocking on the door. It looked like something out of my worst nightmare. Its head was level with my chest and it was covered in snow. Its paws were enormous. It had one of them in mid-air as I pulled back the door and it seemed to leap toward me.

I jumped back out of range and felt a scream rising in my throat. As I stared at it in horror, the thing staggered forward and fell through the doorway.

Then, looking down at it, I realized it was only a gigantic dog.

"Hey, where do you think you're going?" I yelled at it, my terror of a moment before making my voice shake wildly.

It just lay there, whimpering, one back foot still on the outside of the door. Hilary and Daniel came running.

"Ohhh," crooned Hilary, dropping to her knees by

the great beast. "It's Maeve. She went missing the day Mr. Lackland died. Nobody has seen her in over two weeks. Look how thin she is."

I tried to move her mile-long hind leg inside but she was heavy. Then, as I braced myself to try again, she pulled it in herself and I got the door closed, shutting out the stormy night.

She was clearly in a bad way. You could count her ribs easily. Her rough coat was tattered and torn and there were twigs and evergreen bits caught in it. Under a shaggy bang, her amber eyes gazed up at us in mute appeal. They were beautiful eyes.

"She's enormous," Daniel breathed. "What kind of dog is she anyway?"

"Irish wolfhound," Hilary said. "Mr. Lackland was Irish and he'd always wanted one so he bought her just two months before he died. I think she's wonderful."

"She's also starving," Daniel said. "I'll get her something."

His voice sounded uncertain and Hilary took over. Country girls are good at that.

"Warm milk," she said, and ran to the kitchen.

Maeve had to have her head supported when Hilary came back with a large bowl. But, by the time she was halfway through, she had regained enough strength to hold it up for herself. She washed the dish with her great pink tongue. It was as big as a bath towel.

"Are wolfhounds friendly?" Daniel asked, edging back a little.

"She's a darling," Hilary said. "Mr. Lackland spent a fortune on her. My parents thought he was insane but I think she's worth much more than she cost him. Wolfhounds are like the royal dogs in Rosemary Sutcliff's books. Bran and Gelert. You know."

One thing we did have in common with Hilary Wright—all three of us were great readers. We did not go near the TV after that and we forgot all about Faith. Daniel found a juicy steak in the fridge. I cut it into small bits, although not too small since Maeve had a great cave of a mouth.

She wolfhounded it down and actually wagged her tail. It was a feeble effort but clearly heartfelt.

By the time Will's grandfather clock struck ten, we had dried Maeve off and brushed her rough coat. I stared down at her and wondered what to do next. We had promised to go to bed at ten.

"Let's get her upstairs," I said, uncertainly.

She was so weak it took all three of us to get her up the steep flight. When we reached the top and stopped to catch our breath, Daniel said the words that put an end forever to our feud with Hilary.

"She should sleep with you, Hilary," he said. "I can tell that you are the one she wants to be with. Maybe your parents will let you keep her."

"We can help persuade them," I said. "I'll come to give her a boost onto the bed."

At the sight of the spare bed however, Maeve recovered enough strength to spring up onto its comfortable mattress and down quilt. When Will and Mum arrived home, Hilary and Maeve were sound asleep. But, at the first sound of people, Maeve took a flying leap through the air and charged down to defend her new home and mistress. Daniel and I came running to see what would happen.

Hilary's parents were shocked to discover their little daughter had acquired a giant of a dog while they had their backs turned.

"We'll have to take her to the Humane Society," her father said, pulling on his lip. "Although who would want a brute like that I can't imagine."

"Hilary would," I said. "And Maeve wants Hilary too. Look at her."

Hilary, her eyes wide, had sunk down on the bottom step of the stairs and not said a word. Maeve leaned against Hilary's knee and let her big head rest on her new friend's lap. Her head was bigger than the lap it rested on.

As Hilary sent me a look of wonder and thanksgiving, Mum joined in. My mother is a powerful persuader. She told them Hilary needed a friend her own size.

"We have a dog," Mr. Wright started. "He'd be jealous."

"That's the trouble," Daniel said. "YOU have a dog. He's not Hilary's. He's always with you."

"That's perfectly true, Harold," Mrs. Wright said, looking at Daniel with astonishment.

Before her father finally caved in, we had all done

our part to persuade him. Will quietly put in his two cents worth, which also helped. Maeve went home with them and, except for when Hilary is at school, has never left her side since.

On Monday morning, when the three of us got on the bus, Jed Turner called out, "Watch out. Here come the sissy city boys."

Hilary turned on him as though she herself had never once thought such a thing, let alone said it to our faces.

"Dave and Dan are MY cousins," she blazed. "That makes them country kids. So shut up, you brain-dead lout."

Will talks like that. She sounded just like him.

Jed shut up. Everyone shut up. A few days later, we even brought S.P. to school to show the class what an African pygmy hedgehog looks like. Nobody insulted her. They, like Hilary, were jealous.

Being a country boy is fine. And, next Saturday, Mum is driving Hilary, Jed, Nick Wells and the two of us in to tour the Science Centre. Even though she's married to Will, our mum is A-okay. It looks like being a great spring break.

Blahs

Today is a bleak, blank blob of a day,
Lumpy, grumpy, glum and grey.
There's nothing at all that I want to do
And nothing for me to look forward to.
Oh, I know full well I should not complain.
I'm alive and young and free from pain.
The sky is blue and the sun is out
And God's in her heaven, without a doubt.
Days can't constantly veer and vary.
Sometimes things have to be ordinary.
Life is earnest and life is real.
But flat and dismal is how I feel.
Duty has planted a dusty hedge
And I can't see over tomorrow's edge.
Self-pity is boring, exceedingly.
Who cares? I still feel sorry for me.
I've work to do and I'll get it done
But not for one moment will it be fun.
Somebody, save me. Somebody, please,
Come to my rescue. I'm on my knees.

"Get busy," you say, "and write a rhyme."
I have. I did. It's a waste of time.
I guess it's hopeless. Scoff who may.
Today's still a bleak, blank blob of a day,
And, though I don't long to be done and dead,
I'll be awfully glad when it's time for bed.

February

Except that the Sun Is Shining

There is nothing to write a poem about
Except that the sun is shining.
There is nothing remarkable in the sky.
Was there always that sweep of blue?
What is it about the wind today?
It could not really be dancing.
The world is the world I've always known
And yet it feels so new.

The voices of children chime like bells
As they hurry out of the schoolyard.
The snow is washed with a golden light.
Why do I want to sing?
Christmas is over, the New Year past
And Easter is still far distant,
So why do I feel it's a holiday
As blithe as the start of spring?

I'm not in love so it can't be that.
I haven't come into a fortune.
I just had a dutiful deed to do

And this morning I got it done.
Because I didn't procrastinate,
Because it is now behind me,
That's why I see the high blue sky
Ablaze with a special sun.

Such a humdrum reason, one deed well done,
Has sent me to walk with wonder.
I am more alive than my usual self.
My spirit has been set free.
There is nothing to write a poem about
Except that all in an instant,
My world, which yesterday was prose,
Today is poetry.

This jubilation will soon be gone.
New duties will make me grumpy.
Each day will appear an obstacle race.
My nerves will knot and hiss.
May I find it then, this moment when
There was nothing to prompt a poem,
Except that I stopped and beheld my world
And couldn't help writing this.

Freddy Frisbee Finds a Home

Freddy Frisbee lived in an orphanage with forty other boys. They shared everything. There was one swing set, one slide, one large vegetable garden and one medium-sized elderly rabbit who hated boys. Since he was a present from one of the Trustees, they couldn't make rabbit pie out of him.

"I want flowers," Freddy Frisbee told the Matron, "and a dog and a cat of my own."

Matron looked into Freddy's shining eyes.

"And you want songs and stories and someone to love you," she said. "If you remember to keep wanting a home like that, Freddy, you will find it someday."

But when Freddy was five, Mrs. Striver came to the orphanage.

"I'll take a nice, clean boy who needs a home," she told Matron.

Freddy heard her.

"How about me?" he asked.

"What's your name?" Mrs. Striver said in a sharp voice.

"I'm Freddy Frisbee," said Freddy.

Mrs. Striver gave him a sour look.

"You'll never amount to anything with a fool name like that," she said. "From now on, your name will be Frederick Striver."

Freddy was too excited to notice how stern she sounded. He raced up to the dormitory and packed his spare set of clothes.

"We'll miss you, Freddy," his friends said.

"I'll miss you too but I'm going to have a home," Freddy told them. "Maybe there's even a dog."

Matron watched her favourite orphan climb into a dilapidated taxi.

"Good luck, Freddy Frisbee," she called after him. "Hold onto your dreams."

Mrs. Striver heard her. She sniffed and rolled up the taxi window.

"Ridiculous," she snorted. "I don't hold with dreaming."

Freddy was gazing at the busy streets they were passing and did not listen. Finally the taxi drew to a stop.

"Hop out, Frederick," said Mrs. Striver.

"Is the garden in the back?" Freddy asked, staring at the bleak, blank house.

"You don't want a garden. Gardeners never amount to anything," said Mrs. Striver. "My husband used to garden before he ran off."

"I'm only five years old," said Freddy. "I want a garden to play in."

"Even five-year-olds can begin to make something of themselves," she snapped. "Your room is in the attic.

Put your things away neatly. Then come down and help me in the kitchen."

That night, Freddy Frisbee was taught how to peel potatoes properly. He had to scrape the plates and do the dishes. There was no dessert.

He soon found he had no time to play. Mrs. Striver expected him to wash not only dishes but floors and windows and vegetables and behind his ears. She got him to carry in groceries and carry out garbage.

Every day, she showed him a picture of her runaway husband who had joined a circus and been eaten by a lion.

"If he'd stayed with me, Frederick, I'd have seen to it that he amounted to something," she said.

In the picture, Freddy saw that Mr. Striver had a tired, sad, grey face. He looked lonely. Freddy hoped he had enjoyed the circus before he became a lion's lunch.

When her adopted son started school, Mrs. Striver told the teacher his name was Frederick Striver. Freddy did not argue. But he asked Patsy Bird who sat next to him to call him Freddy.

"Freddy is a grand name," Patsy said.

Patsy was Freddy's friend for two years. They liked the same songs. Their favourite was "You Are My Sunshine." They loved the same stories. Their favourite was *The Tale of Peter Rabbit*.

"He didn't amount to anything," said Freddy.

"Who cares?" said Patsy. "He had such fun."

Then Patsy's family moved. And Freddy Frisbee was alone.

"May I have a dog?" he asked.

"Dogs are a waste of time and money," Mrs. Striver told him. "Dog owners never amount to anything."

"May I have a cat?" Freddy asked a year later.

"Cats are a waste of money and time," Mrs. Striver said. "I want you to amount to something."

By the time Freddy Frisbee had grown up, his adoptive mother had transformed him. Frederick Striver forgot he had once been Freddy Frisbee. He was a very busy, very rich man with a sad, grey face. He never sang songs. He never read stories. He never thought of Matron or Patsy Bird. He just thought about money.

Mrs. Striver's last words were, "Well, at least you've amounted to something."

Now the bleak, blank house belonged to Frederick Striver alone. He could do what he liked. Yet he didn't think of buying a dog or a cat. He did not plant a garden. All he wanted in a house was no more washing.

He went looking for a place that would take care of itself. He found the very latest thing.

"You can program this house so that it will do what you tell it to," the salesman promised. "Before you get home, you can order it to turn up the heat, turn on the coffee, switch on the lights and the TV. It will even keep itself clean and tidy."

Freddy Frisbee bought the big new house and moved in at once. Every afternoon, at five o'clock exactly, he would get into his car to go home. Then he would pick up a small computer.

"Turn up the heat. Open the garage door. Switch on the coffee. Get the Business News on TV," he'd tell it. Last of all, he'd order his house to clean up everything that needed cleaning. And when he arrived at the front door, the house had done it all.

He should have been overjoyed with such a smart house. But he was miserable. And the house knew it.

One mild day in February, Freddy Frisbee put his key in the lock and turned it. The lock clicked open. Then, before he could twist the doorknob, it clicked shut. Freddy tried again. It happened just as before. His house had locked him out.

Freddy tried and tried. It was no use. He could not get into his own house. He went to a window and peered in.

The house had not switched on the coffee. It had made itself a pot of tea. The house had not turned on the business news. It was watching *Reading Rainbow*. Even though the wind was chilly, the house had not turned up the heat. It had made itself a little fire in the grate. And the house was humming.

Freddy stood still and listened. He knew the tune but he could not quite remember the words. Yet, all at once, he felt five years old.

He left his car in the garage. He walked down the country road where his house stood. He climbed a hill and turned down a winding lane. The bare tree branches whispered over his head. The golden sun was beginning to set and a silver sliver of moon was rising. Freddy Frisbee saw his first star in years.

I have nowhere to sleep. I should be worrying, thought Freddy. I should be making plans. I ought to be sensible.

Instead, he began to whistle softly.

Then he saw a house. It was not a big new house like his. It looked slapdash and ramshackle and happy-go-lucky. Warm light spilled through the downstairs windows. Smoke curled from the chimney. Snowdrops and winter aconite were pushing through the snow on the protected south side. Inside, someone was singing.

"You are my sunshine," sang the voice.

Freddy stood still and listened. Weren't those the words he had been trying to remember?

A big dog came to greet him, wagging its tail. It turned and led the way up the path. Freddy followed it as though they were old friends.

An orange cat was curled up on the porch swing. It jumped down and walked to the door and scratched with its paw. The singing stopped.

"I'm coming, Purrcy," said a voice.

Freddy stared at the door. There was something familiar about that voice. Then a woman looked out.

"Hello, Freddy Frisbee," she said.

Freddy blinked. He was sure he had seen that freckled nose, that big smile and those green eyes before.

"I heard you'd moved into that strange place up the

road," she went on. "I just baked a pie to take to you. Not rabbit. Come on in. Supper's ready."

Freddy followed her, feeling as though he were in the middle of a dream. The cat led him to a big rocking chair. In it lay a small book. Freddy picked it up and saw that it was *The Tale of Peter Rabbit*.

"You're Patsy Bird," Freddy Frisbee said.

"Of course," she answered, grinning exactly like the five-year-old who had been his friend.

He stayed for supper. He and Patsy talked until the moon was high in the sky. They went for a walk around the garden. Freddy saw that the snow was melting. Then they were quiet together.

"I want to sing," Freddy blurted out.

"Let's," said Patsy.

She started them off but it only took him a minute to be brave enough to join in.

Freddy Frisbee sold his fancy house. He gave the key to the buyer. He never went back inside even though it had been the house that had set him free.

"I'm grateful to that house," he told Patsy. "If it hadn't locked me out, I might never have found you."

"I'd have come with my pie," said Patsy Bird. "Come on home, Freddy Frisbee."

Valentine

As the hive holds the honey,
As the cage holds the dove,
As the mint holds the money,
My heart holds love.

As the road loves the rover,
As the bird loves the blue,
As the bee loves the clover,
My heart loves you.

While my head holds a poem,
While my heart holds a song,
While my hand holds a pencil,
I'll love you that long.

Through bliss and through boredom,
Through singing and sorrow,
Through all my todays
And through every tomorrow.

Gardeners

The teacher is making our class grow a bean.
We're waiting and waiting for it to turn green.
A book that we read said it soon would have roots
And, almost at once, it would sprout up green shoots.
It's in a glass jar behind a wet blotter.
It has the best fresh air and sunshine and water.
My mother says talking to plants helps them grow,
So whenever I'm near it, I tell it, "Hello."
A little white lump, though, is all we have seen.
Tomorrow I'm reading the book to the bean.

The Night of the Next Straw

One day, when I was coming in the door, I heard Dad say, "That's the last straw."

For a second, I thought he was talking about drinking straws and he meant we had run out of them. Then I knew that was not it and I remembered the other kind of straw. It was dried grass, something like hay, only more prickly. I looked around for some. But there was no straw anywhere. I was curious but I could tell that Dad was mad about something so I went and asked Ma.

"What's 'the last straw' mean?" I said.

Ma pushed back her long hair and went on cleaning out the refrigerator.

"With mothers, there's no such thing," she muttered. "They load on the last straw and, before the camel has time to collapse, they put on the next straw and tell her to keep moving. There's always a next straw and one more desert to cross."

I stared at her. How did a camel get into it?

She glanced at me and laughed. Then she shut the refrigerator door and sat down at the kitchen table. She

196

sipped her lukewarm coffee while she thought.

"It comes from a story or an expression about there being only a certain load of straw a camel can carry," she explained. "If they put on one too many, the camel can't bear it. 'That's the last straw,' he growls. Then he sinks down on the sand and refuses to budge."

"What did you say about mothers?" I pressed her.

"Jonah, get thee behind me with such interesting questions," she said. "I have work to do."

"I didn't know camels growled," I told her as she finished the coffee and headed back to the things that had gone mouldy.

"Well, this one can," she said. "So go and play with your baby brother before HE, too, decides to ask me something I don't know."

Seth is only five, but I like playing with him. He's a neat kid. Still I kept wondering what Ma meant about "the next straw." And, after the night I'm going to tell about was over, I thought I understood. Ever since, I've called it "the night of the next straw."

Before I tell what happened, I want to say that we are a happy family. We argue and sometimes even yell at each other. But, deep down, we are glad we are related. We wouldn't trade with anyone else, even the ones whose parents buy them whatever they want. That's what made it so amazing the night my mother took off right at suppertime.

It was Sunday night and we were starting to eat when it happened. My father's parents had come for dinner and my grandmother Margie had just told my fifteen-year-old sister Judith to stop showing off.

Margie (she hates us calling her Grandma) puts on this sugary smile when she tells us off. She pretends she is joking but everyone knows she's really telling Ma and Dad that they should be bringing us up better.

"Our mother always taught us," old Margie cooed nastily, "that children should not be allowed to monopolize the conversation. I'm sure we're all pleased that you're so good at sports, Judith dear, but haven't you gone on about it a little too long? I'm sure your mother wishes you would let your grandpa get a word in about his interests."

Grandpa was stuffing his face with Ma's cabbage rolls and he didn't even look up. He hardly ever speaks unless you are alone with him. All he says, most times, is, "Pass the butter, Jonah," or "We have to go home now."

I saw Ma's face tighten and Judith opened her mouth to fight back and then Seth looked down at the stir-fry and said, "Yuck, yuck, yuck!" The next instant, I squeezed the ketchup bottle so hard that ketchup splurted out all over everything, including the clean tablecloth Ma had gotten out for the company. One big blob actually landed on the sleeve of the Erin knit sweater Dad gave her for her birthday.

I don't usually do things like that but I was so fed up with Margie that I strangled the ketchup. There was one frozen second before my father laughed.

Then, as if his laugh was a signal, Ma stood up, looked at all of us as though she were seeing us for the first time and didn't like what she saw, and, without a word, she walked out of the room.

Behind her, everyone began yelling at everyone else. Nobody noticed me put down the ketchup carefully and slide off my chair to follow her.

I don't know what I thought I could do to fix things. Maybe I meant to apologize about the ketchup. Maybe I just could not stand hearing my sister say, for the millionth time, "Jonah was certainly the right name for you." I can't be sure now. But as I reached the hall, I saw the front door swing shut. It didn't quite slam but it shut with a thud that meant business. She was mad. I didn't blame her. Sometimes even happy families are an almighty pain in the butt.

I need to explain our family before I forget. I'm the middle one and adopted. They wanted Judith to have a brother and when she was five and they thought no brother was coming, they got me. My birth father was native and my birth mother white. That makes me a dark white. I like the way I look.

Then, when I was five, along came the brother they had planned to have earlier.

"Why did you keep me when you got Seth?" I asked Ma one time.

"I'd gotten used to having you around," she said. "You were a bad habit I couldn't break."

You might think that was a terrible thing to say. But

Ma has this crooked grin that tells me she's joking. We usually understand each other.

"Well, if you ever get sick of me, just give me a hint and I'll run away," I told her.

"It's a deal, Jonah," she said.

Then she was the one who ran.

When I was five or six, Judith told me I couldn't really be a true Indian because I sounded like an elephant when I walked.

"Everybody in the whole world knows that true Indians walk without making a sound," she said.

She was crazy, of course, but I believed her for long enough that I taught myself to walk nearly silently. It has come in handy many times. So, although I now know Indians walk just like everybody else, I knew I could shadow my mother without her hearing a footfall or twig snapping or snow crunching.

We live in a small town called Fergus, Ontario, in a stone house on St. David Street. We moved here from Hamilton three years ago because Seth's asthma was bad there.

I was only about twenty seconds behind my mother. I was closing the door when I caught sight of her polar fleece jacket hanging on its hook. Even though she had on that thick sweater, she would have put the jacket on over it if she had not been too mad to think straight. I grabbed it and sprinted after her as silently as any true Indian.

Luckily, I was in time to see her turn right off St.

David and stride away down Hill Street.

I slung the jacket over my shoulder and, as I felt the nip in the air, was pleased I'd brought it. Ma shivers when I'm roasting so I knew she'd soon feel cold. I had on a sweater and coat so I was warmer than warm. I didn't think I should run to catch up with her until she calmed down some so I just matched my pace to hers. I had to jog. She was really moving.

She went down the hill and then started up the next. As she neared Tower Street, she slowed. It was then I saw that I was not the only one shadowing her. Our calico cat, Pluperfect, was accompanying her in a zig-zag way, pretending she was out all by herself but keeping up beautifully.

Ma turned left on Tower Street. So did Pluperfect. So did I.

Then Ma spotted the cat who was making so much noise, pouncing and bouncing, clearly not a true Indian.

Ma halted.

"Who asked you to come along, cat?" she growled. "Or are you leaving for your own reasons?"

Pluperfect gave her a sidewise glance and then began staring up a tree where a squirrel was frisking about.

My mother tossed her head and went on walking. Pluperfect instantly lost interest in the squirrel and shot after her again.

I took a chance and got closer as I heard Ma begin talking.

She started by swearing. I didn't know she knew all those words. Then she kept talking, the words coming out in furious spurts.

"I slave all day at the school. Then I come home and cook a good dinner. And he lets his parents come over to make snide remarks while they fill their faces. Not once has he defended me against that old . . . ferret."

She stopped walking for a second as though she were listening to what she had just said. Then she hugged herself to keep warm and gave a little snort of laughter.

I nearly blew my cover by laughing too. My grandmother is long and skinny with white hair and reddish eyes. She sniffs a lot. She is exactly like a ferret. My friend Nick has a ferret and it is her twin. It looks peaceful until the instant before it bites. Margie can get things out of you too, make you tell her things you don't mean to. Then she quotes you when it'll make the most trouble.

Ma marched on, still muttering.

"Why didn't I just go up and shut myself in the bedroom?" she asked the cat, who was sniffing a suspicious bush. "Because I didn't want to be in the same house with them for another second! That's why."

I was wondering whether I should come out of hiding and hand over the jacket and tell her I was sorry about spilling the ketchup when she spoke my name. I kept still and stretched my ears to their utmost.

"Poor old Jonah!" she said, and I could hear she was

smiling a little. "He didn't mean to set me off. He's my kindred spirit. Judith, on the other hand, bores me almost as much as she bores her grandmother. And if I hear Seth call something I cook "yucky" one more time, I'll wash his mouth out with laundry soap even if it kills him."

She marched ahead another half-block. Then she stood and looked around as though she sensed someone was watching and she was afraid it might be some tattletale, nosy person like Margie. Nobody but Pluperfect was in sight, however, since I was well hidden behind a large tree trunk. Neither of us could be sure, though, who was peering out through the nearby windows. That must have been what made her suddenly speak a few words in a loud voice which she tried to make sound off-hand and easy.

"I need to rest my feet," she remarked to nobody. "These shoes are killing me. I'll go and sit on a tombstone for a minute before I go home."

That was good news. While she was watching the cat, I dropped her jacket over the wall and got over myself into the Auld Kirk graveyard behind St. Andrew's Presbyterian Church. It is one of my favourite places in Fergus. Everybody buried there has been there for such a long time, you can wonder about them in a peaceful way. This time, instead of wandering about thinking, I ducked down behind the big stone closest to the wall, held my breath and listened to see if Ma had spotted me.

She opened the gate, came through and walked over to the big flat stone straight in front of her. She looked down before she sat and said, "Thank you, William Rennie, for letting me rest in peace."

Then there was this silence. It seemed to go on for hours. Ma stared down at her runners, which were far too light for the cold evening and brooded. I could tell it was going to take a while even though I knew she must be shivering.

I settled myself more comfortably to wait her out. The cat came over the wall too, nosed me lightly, and sauntered on closer. Then she touched Ma's ankle with her nose, did one of her weaving cat dances around Ma's feet. She jumped away when Ma called her. She is only interested in laps when it is her own idea. She especially likes curling up on top of you just before you are going to stand up.

"I'm waiting for a sign," Ma told her. "Surely one of these stones will give me a word from on high."

Then she was quiet again. While she stared off into space, I got up, sneaked to the gate and hung the jacket where she could not possibly miss it. Nobody else's coat looks like it. It was mostly yellow until Seth coloured it one day with non-washable markers. When she looked up, I was safely hidden behind another big stand-up grave marker, closer to William Rennie's. I wanted to hear better.

A couple of minutes dragged by. I peeked out and saw she was now examining the stone right in front of her. It was the only one in the graveyard made of red stone instead of grey. As she read it, she laughed.

"That's pretty plain," she said. "Thank goodness, because I'm freezing. Let's go, puss."

She rose and turned to go out the gate. There was a long moment as she stood looking at her own jacket hanging there. I sucked in my breath.

"Jonah," she said. "It's got to be Jonah."

She put the jacket on and hugged it close and then, half-running, she headed up Tower Street.

The minute she was almost out of sight, I dashed to the stone she had been reading.

IN MEMORY OF GEORGE
DIED MAY 2, 1851   AGE 32
ELDEST SON OF ANDREW CLEPHANE, ESQ.
LATE SHERIFF OF FIFESHIRE SCOTLAND

brother of the author of "The Ninety and Nine"

What on earth...? Confused, but in too big a hurry to think, I scrambled over the wall and ran myself, sure Ma wasn't noticing noises any longer.

Before we got back to the house, my grandparents had been packed off home. Seth and Judith had been sent to their rooms. The dishwasher had been loaded. And my dad had come out on the porch to look for us.

Then he spotted Ma.

She stopped and waited to see what he would say.

But he did not speak a word, not at first. He just ran down the steps and hugged her hard. Then he told her how he had sorted everything out.

"Come on in," he said. "I'll nuke us some dinner."

Ma turned and looked for me. I guess the jacket had told her I must be somewhere around. I had not made a sound. Now I stepped forward. She just smiled and stretched out her hand, pulling me in.

"I knew it was you," she said.

I didn't need to answer. Dad didn't even notice us. He was too busy bragging how he had settled everything while we'd been gone. He was proud of himself and I could see why. Yet Ma does that kind of thing every day. Straw after straw. Desert after desert.

I told her that, when she came up to say goodnight. She laughed.

"My desert is plentifully supplied with oases," she said. "Sleep well, Boy Who Brings Coats to Cold Camels."

I had fetched the old hymnbook out of the piano bench. After Ma had gone, I turned the light back on and looked up Clephane, Elizabeth. She had two hymns in the book but it was easy to pick the right one. It told the story of the lost sheep and how the good Shepherd goes through all sorts of dangers to find it. The last verse must have been the one with the message.

And all through the mountains, thunder-riven,
And up from the rocky steep,

There rose a cry to the gate of heaven,
"Rejoice, I have found My sheep."
And the angels echoed around the throne,
"Rejoice for the Lord brings back His own.
Rejoice for the Lord brings back His own."

I laughed when I got it. But I felt sort of like crying too. Ma would have come home anyway, I knew. But I was glad the poem told her how we would rejoice. For she is definitely our own.

Since then, I've been careful with the ketchup bottle. Seth has not said "yuck" about the food either. I warned him what might happen. As for Judith, she's still boring but my father doesn't let her blather on so long. Best of all, my grandmother no longer comes EVERY Sunday. I don't know how Dad did it but she waits to be invited. All of us kids call Granny "The Ferret" now. Behind her back, of course, and when Ma can't hear either. It's perfect.

I didn't tell anybody the bit about the two of us being kindred spirits. I think about it though. I feel the same way about Ma. I don't think she is a camel. I don't believe she's a sheep either. She for sure is no ferret.

I know. I'll adopt HER.

Lady

I heard you prattling the other day.
"I'm a perfect lady," I heard you say.
Such blatant falsehoods cause me pain.
Listen closely while I explain.
"Lady" comes from centuries back.
It's Anglo-Saxon, to be exact.
Early Britons joined "loaf" and "dig"
And created "lady." Now do you twig?
A lady isn't just one of the girls
With a perm and a pout and a pile of curls.
A lady is someone who kneads the dough,
Sets it to rise, then bakes it slow.
Get this into your empty head.
Since you're a broad who bakes no bread,
You ain't no lady. What's more, I can
Say "Hey, lady!" and mean a man.

My dad, an overworked M.D.,
WAS a perfect lady occasionally.
Every so often, on Saturday morning,
He'd roll up his sleeves, without any warning,

And announce that he was about to start
Making some bread. Mum played no part.
Knowing he might have only an hour,
He'd fly around in a flurry of flour,
Then he'd punch the dough, all light with leaven,
And, while it was baking, it smelled like heaven.
The dismal day grew fair instead
Warmed by the smell of my dad's fresh bread.

An impatient fellow was my father.
Wanting the bread without the bother
Of waiting for dough to rise, he'd set
The pans on the rad. Soon he would get
The punched-down loaves to rise up quickly.
We'd snatch hot slices, spread butter thickly
And wolf down every scrumptious bite.
We all knew that, tomorrow night,
If we tried some more of his homemade bread
It would sit in our stomachs like lumps of lead.
Even the birds who ate the crumbs
Felt a heaviness in their tums
And, however they flapped their feathers, found
They weighed too much to get off the ground.
We downed Dad's bread while it was hot
And teased him later. But he did not
Give up trying despite our laughter.
I hope he is baking, in the hereafter,
Sky-high loaves to make God glad,
My loveable, laughable, ladylike dad.

March

Speaking of Stars

This poem is not linked to a season unless you say it's a celebration of the March Equinox, when the Sun starts returning to the Northern Hemisphere the hours winter has stolen.

The star that gives to us our day
Waves the universe away,
Scoffs at all astronomy
Has taught us, claims that only she
Shines in the heavens. "If they're bent
On sharing my blue firmament,
Why can't I see one? It's derisible.
If they were up here, they'd be visible.
And while this Sun beams, smugly bright,
Proud as a peacock of her light,
The galaxies, in silence, burn,
Waiting for the earth to turn
And set our dazzled vision free
To contemplate infinity.
The great stars are above debating
One medium star's performance rating.
It is beneath their dignity

To vent their fire on such as she,
Who can't be made to recognize
Her lack of consequence and size.
They see she's made the old mistake
Of peering into every lake,
Every puddle, trough and pond,
Until she has grown far too fond
Of her own face reflected there.
She has forgotton one must stare
Away from self, if one would see
One's actual luminosity.

A star with no sense of her station
Forfeits her right to veneration.
Our Sun compels us to remind her
That we've glimpsed myriad stars—behind her.
Egyptians used to prostrate lie
When they beheld her in the sky.
They made her male and called her god.
No wonder her perspective's flawed.
Such lunacy should be corrected.
It's time the sunrise was neglected.
Let's give our wondering exclamations
To greater stars, in constellations,
Till our Sun comes to recognize
She's middle-aged and medium size.
The Sun, though, has her sphere. If she
Forsook us, we would cease to be.
No other star in the vast train

Would fill our lungs with breath again
It ill behooves us to be rude
And scorn her gifts of warmth and food.
We should instead give her applause
For the kind nurturing she does.
We live our lives because her face is
Turned toward us on a daily basis.
If it were left to me to choose
The far stars or the near, I'd lose
No time in making my decision.
Vitality comes first, then vision.

One final point deserves attention.
Our Sun has arts I've failed to mention.
Though other stars each light a spark
Illumining the endless dark
For poets and philosophers,
Our Sun has gifts uniquely hers.
They are less lofty, less eternal,
For she, praise be, remains diurnal.
Our Sun, so silly and so vain,
Discovers prisms in the rain
And loops a bow of colours fair
Through the grey of our despair,
Making a miracle of grace
Shine on us from the commonplace.

Somebody's Girl

When a truck smashed into their car on the way to Rose's ballet class, Mum was killed and Rose was badly hurt. She was in hospital for weeks. She was still there when Grandma moved in to take care of Dad and Pippa.

Dad came to visit Rose in the evenings. But he never knew what to say. Sometimes she pretended to go to sleep so he could tiptoe out. One night, she overheard him talking to someone in the corridor.

"It's so good of my mother to come, Mary," he said. "Pippa took one look at her and stopped being a lost soul. She's no longer having those nightmares. She and Mother are as thick as thieves."

"What wonderful news!" Mary Gilchrist's voice answered. Mary had been Mum's best friend since they were young and now she was a special friend of Rose's, too, because she was a children's librarian. Whenever Rose had had free time, before the accident, she had either danced or read a book. She opened her mouth to call out a greeting when she heard Mary speak again.

"How is Rose, Blair? Will she be able to walk normally when she leaves here?"

Rose held her breath. She knew the answer by now. No matter how hard she worked in therapy, her left foot dragged. She would always limp and she would never dance again. She had fought against the knowledge at first but, just the day before, she had faced the therapist and asked, "I'll always limp, won't I?"

Miss Fraser had hesitated but finally she had nodded. She had gone on to talk about how important it was for Rose to keep on exercising but Rose had not listened. Dad must know too. But he had not once spoken to her about it. She strained to hear what he would say. But he lowered his voice. Unable to catch more than a mumble, Rose lay back, trying not to cry.

Thick as thieves, she thought. That's the right word. Grandma is a thief. She's stolen Mum's place and now she's stealing my sister. I won't learn to dance now either.

A small inner voice told her that it was a good thing Grandma was there since Pippa was only four. Pippa, without Mum or Rose, sounded like someone marooned on a desert island. Grandma walking in the door and holding out her arms must have seemed like the rescue ship coming at last.

Dad's voice rose as he went back to talking about Pippa. She had flung herself into Grandma's arms and burst into a storm of tears.

"When I said that was no way to welcome her

grandmother," he went on, "Mother said, 'Let her be. She has lots to cry about.'"

Rose, listening once more, longed to throw things. How dare Grandma be at home comforting Pippa while she, Rose, was stuck in hospital? It wasn't fair. It wasn't right.

Three months after the accident, on a blustery March afternoon, Rose came home. As she limped out the door of the hospital, a gust of wind caught at her and made her shiver. March or no March, spring was a long way off. She felt cold to her bones.

When they reached home, Dad helped her out of the car. She stumbled, momentarily off balance.

"I'll carry you, Posy," he said, reaching for her.

Rose knew it hurt him to have to watch her dragging her bad foot. She gave him a savage look.

"I'll walk," she said, sounding far older than ten. "You'll have to get used to it. And don't call me Posy."

"I'm sorry, Rose," Dad's voice was gruff. "I guess you are getting too old for Posy."

He had forgotten where the nickname had come from. She was glad. She could not bear to talk about it. When they got to the house, he held the door open for her. Rose took a deep breath and hobbled into the hall.

Grandma was waiting there. She and Pippa had come to visit a couple of times but Rose had always been in bed. At the sight of her granddaughter's struggle to walk, her eyes filled with quick tears and she cried out, "Oh, you poor little thing!"

"I am NOT a 'poor little thing,'" Rose ground out through set teeth.

At the look in her blazing eyes, Grandma involuntarily backed up a step. Then she tried to repair the damage.

"Forgive me, darling," she said hastily. "It was a shock. I couldn't help remembering your dancing . . . It hurts me to see you this way."

Ever since she had faced the truth about her limp, Rose had been fighting off her own memories of ballet classes and recitals. She had been having dancing lessons since she was Pippa's age. Her favourite book was her mother's old copy of *Ballet Shoes*. Posy, the youngest of the three Fossil sisters in the book, had been the born dancer. When Rose talked of nothing but dancing and practised all the time, her mother had begun calling her Posy. Even her dance teacher said she showed "real promise."

Grandma's words struck at Rose's defences like rocks hurled at a glass wall. Then and there, her bruised heart declared war on the woman she had always loved before.

I'll be polite to you, she thought, staring at Grandma's tear-wet face in stony silence. But I'll never love you again. Pippa can be your darling, not me.

That night, alone in her room, Rose pushed the battered copy of *Ballet Shoes* behind the others on the shelf where she kept her favourite books. She turned the light out fast before she had a chance to see the rest. Almost all of them had been gifts from her mother. *The Secret Garden* was there, and *My Friend Flicka*, *Emily of New Moon* and *Nobody's Girl*. Even in the darkness, she could picture the line of familiar spines. She had to have them near. But not *Ballet Shoes* or Rumer Godden's *Thursday's Children*.

Arming her heart against Grandma's pity and holding off her concern gave Rose something to concentrate on in the first difficult days. Several times, she caught herself wishing she were still safe in hospital. She had hated it there but the routine had been predictable and nobody had expected her to be the Rose she had been before the accident.

Yet she did love being back in her own bedroom and, most of the time, she loved being with her little sister.

If only they would stop treating her like a guest! And if only she did not miss her mother so terribly.

The other three had had time to adjust to Mum's not being there but Rose still expected her to walk into the kitchen or come running down the stairs. She listened for Mum's voice too. Mum was always singing. Now the house was as quiet as death.

Other things had changed as well.

"Where's the old sugar bowl?" Rose demanded at breakfast. Pippa looked away. She blushed.

"It got lost," she said too quickly. "Isn't this one pretty?"

Rose glanced at the new sugar bowl. It was fine but not the one she was used to.

"I like the old one. Mum had it ever since I was a baby," she said stiffly.

"I think this is loads nicer," Pippa insisted, still not meeting Rose's gaze. "Grandma found it. It has a cream pitcher to match it."

Pippa jumped up then and ran out of the room. Grandma, busy at the counter, sent a rueful glance after her and Rose suddenly knew that Pippa must have broken the old sugar bowl. Probably Grandma had found the pieces.

Why didn't she make Pippa confess? Mum thought telling the truth was important.

"Here's your hot chocolate, Rose," her grandmother said, putting it next to Rose. "I'm sorry about the bowl."

Rose looked at the mug. Grandma had given it to her years ago. It had her initial on it. Pippa had one too. Rose studied hers while she waited for Grandma to make Pippa tell the truth. When Grandma sat down instead and sipped her coffee, Rose watched her own hand knock against her mug, sending it crashing to the floor.

Grandma leaped up.

"Never mind, Rose. Accidents happen. Don't move," she ordered. "Let me get the bits before you cut yourself."

Pippa, eyes wide, rushed to the door and peered in.

"Stay there, Pippa," Grandma waved her away. She stooped and began gathering up the shattered china in a bunched paper towel.

Rose looked on. She felt very far away. She felt as though she could not move if she tried.

This is what turning to stone must feel like, she told herself.

"Rose, ease up on your grandmother," Dad said later. "Where would we be without her? She's given up her home to come and look after us."

"We don't need her," Rose muttered. "We could manage ourselves now I'm back. I could stay home from school. They'd send a teacher."

"You will go back to school on Monday," he said. "I'll drive you if necessary. Don't change the subject, Rose. We could not manage without your grandmother and you know it. You are giving her a hard time."

"I'm never rude to her," Rose defended herself.

"Politeness is pretty cold comfort," her father said. "She loves you, child. Can't you see that?"

Rose looked away from Dad's worried eyes. He did not understand. Nobody did.

She loves Pippa, she thought. She doesn't need me.

She went on being coolly polite to Grandma. But keeping it up was hard. Often, she felt the wall between them starting to crumble. Grandma was trying so hard not to hurt Rose's feelings. But Rose hung onto one stabbing memory which had returned to her after the accident.

Mum had been talking once to Mary about Grandma.

"Blair's mother puts up with me but she has never,

for one moment, thought me worthy of her precious boy. I'm sure she still believes he made a dire mistake marrying me."

"Nonsense!" Mary had said. "She thinks you're great."

But what if it weren't nonsense? If Grandma really thought Mum was not the right wife for Dad, Rose should not forgive her. Even though Grandma was being kind, Rose knew she must hold out against that kindness whatever Dad said.

Sometimes she even had to lie in order to escape. Pippa caught her. She did not tattle but she said, "You shouldn't tell Grandma fibs."

Rose thought of the "lost" sugar bowl but she did not bring it up. Lying was wrong. Both Mum and Dad had told her the fable of The Boy Who Cried Wolf so often that Rose was pleased that the wolves got the little wimp in the end. Since the accident, however, Dad rarely scolded Rose. Instead, he treated her as though she were made of china. Even when she brought home a bad report card, he acted as though the low grades were the teacher's fault, not Rose's.

Grandma was tougher. She had called Rose "a poor little thing" that once but she knew her granddaughter much better by now.

"Get to work, Rose," she said after Dad had gone out. "You are slacking off and you know it. Don't count on them taking pity on you. You'll end up despising yourself. That's no way to live."

Rose seethed with fury. Knowing Grandma was right made it worse. She clumped off without answering. At breakfast next morning, Rose ate half her porridge and felt full. When Grandma was not looking, she tipped what was left into the garbage.

"Did you finish your oatmeal, Rose?" Grandma asked.

Why did she have to choose this morning to ask?

"Yes," Rose mumbled. "Of course."

Grandma gave her a slice of toast, passed the jam and, five minutes later, discovered the porridge in the garbage.

"Rose, have you heard of The Boy Who Cried Wolf?" she asked.

"Yes!" Rose yelled, putting her hands over her ears. "Yes, I've heard about him so much he makes me sick. Don't tell me about him. Don't!"

If Dad had been there, she would have been in big trouble. Grandma's hands shook and she turned away. Her silence made Rose squirm.

"All right, child. Maybe it needed more salt," Grandma said finally in a husky voice. "Hurry or you'll be late."

She left the room. Rose ate her toast and watched the door. But her grandmother did not come back. Rose actually thought of saying she was sorry. She mustn't turn to mush though. After school, she would go to the library and see Mary. Mary always understood and sympathized.

Rose did not tell Grandma she was going. She

hated people knowing where she was every minute.

If I tell her stuff, she fumed silently, she'll want me to run an errand. I have to get away or I'll explode.

On the way out, Rose left her library books in a tote bag in the empty umbrella stand inside the front door. She planned to ease the door open after school, fish them out, drop her backpack and be gone before anyone knew she had come. Dad would not be home yet. Nobody would notice she was late. And she would be quick. She knew just the books she wanted.

She was almost home, watching for icy patches which might make her fall, when she heard Pippa call her name. Rose's head jerked up.

Trust her to ruin things, she thought, waving.

"Hi, Pip," she called. Pippa was so comical with her wild curls escaping from her hood, her round glasses sliding off her button nose and her big grin. Rose loved her. But she still did not want to take her along. Even though the library was public property, Rose felt the children's department was her own private kingdom. She loved the big bright room upstairs with its shelves and shelves of treasures yet to be discovered. She also loved being with Mary, who told Rose which new books to try first.

Pippa ran to Rose. She was still dressed for winter even though she had tried to make Grandma let her go to school without mittens or boots this morning. She had her boots on and they were even on the right feet. Her mittens dangled from her pockets but they matched.

"I'm coming too," she announced happily, taking Rose's hand in icy fingers.

"Put your mitts on. Coming where?" Rose asked, doing her best to sound casual.

"To the library. Where else?" Pippa said, ignoring the part about mitts.

"What makes you think I'm going there?" Rose demanded, scowling.

"Grandma and I found your books in the umbrella stand," Pippa said triumphantly. "You always put them there when—"

"But you can't even read," Rose broke in, furious at them for uncovering her hiding place.

"You can read to me," Pippa said. "And I can look at picture books."

"Did you ask . . . ?" Rose began. She stopped. Grandma knew.

"Grandma helped me get ready," Pippa said patiently. "She gave me her books to bring back too and a note for Mary. She said, 'Don't hurry back.'"

Rose stared at the smaller girl in surprise.

"But . . . but . . ." she sputtered.

"Come on, Rose. You carry the bag. It's heavy."

Rose took the bag and started to limp along. Neither girl noticed the limp now. Pippa had confided in Rose once that she was the only big sister who didn't keep saying, "Hurry up!" all the time.

As they neared the library, Rose wondered briefly about what Grandma was doing. She minded Pippa after kindergarten got out. Rose had often imagined them having fun together while she was stuck in math class. She had never been asked to return Grandma's books before.

"The fresh air does me good," Grandma always said.

It was puzzling. But not important. Rose let it slip her mind as she thought over which books to choose this time. She always got one book she had read before in case the new ones were disappointing. Maybe she would reread *Tom's Midnight Garden* or *The Minerva Program*.

Rose shifted the book bag to her left hand and frowned.

"What was Grandma doing when you left?" she asked.

"Grandma? What was she doing?" Pippa repeated. She sounded completely blank, as though Rose had spoken to her in a foreign language. "What do you mean?"

"Oh, Pip, use your brain. Was she baking or dusting or what?"

"She was going upstairs," Pippa said. "She was pulling herself up by the bannister and saying, 'I think I can. I think I can.' Like The Little Engine That Could."

"I know who said it," Rose said, her tone sharpening. "What was she going to do upstairs?"

"She said she'd lie down. Her ankle hurt. She was walking like you."

Rose remembered vaguely that their grandmother had slipped on the ice the day before and twisted her ankle. Rose had not paid much attention. Grandma had made dinner as usual so it couldn't have hurt much, could it? Rose surely would have seen if Grandma had been in pain. But . . .

"We're here," Pippa darted to the big front door.

Rose could have taken the elevator. They had showed her how to find it and make it work. It was not near the door from outside though and only certain people were allowed to use it. It made Rose feel embarrassed. It was not what regular people did if they were able to manage the stairs. Rose could manage. She started up. Pippa waited on the landing. Rose toiled up the second flight. On the top step, she put down the books and rested.

"Come OK, Posy!"

Rose blinked, then smiled a little. Even Pippa had stopped using the old nickname. It sounded nice. Smiling, she heaved up the bag and went to the desk. Mary was busy so she left the books and went to look for new ones. She got *Awake and Dreaming*, *JYP*, *The Moor Child*, *Ramona the Brave* and *From Anna*. A girl at school had said it was great. Rose carried her stack to the desk.

Mary was free. As Rose got out the books Grandma was returning, a sealed envelope fell to the floor. Rose picked it up. Why had Grandma sealed it shut? When she sent a note to Rose's teacher, she just tucked in the flap. MARY was written on it.

"Hi, Rose. Is that for me?" Mary asked, smiling.

Rose smiled back and handed it over. The librarian scanned the note. When she was halfway through, she sobered and shot Rose a searching glance. She started to speak, hesitated and then put the page down.

"I'll get her books," she said. "I won't be long."

Just before she strode away, she moved the letter so that it was face up where Rose would be sure to see it. As she vanished into the stacks, her face was pink and her back very straight.

Rose stared after her. Mary meant her to read what Grandma had written. But Grandma herself had stuck down the flap of the envelope. Unsure of what to do, Rose glanced down and caught sight of her own name. That settled it. She began to read.

Dear Mary,

I've twisted my ankle so I'm sending my books back with Rose and Pippa. I need to get away and I need books to take me. I love the girls but even so I have to escape or I'd go mad. Give me some old favourites. I want a story I can depend on.

The Blue Castle would be ideal. I'd love to read *Nobody's Girl* again but I'm sure you don't have such an old book. After all, I read it when I was a child "in the olden days" as Pippa says. I bought one second-hand but it disappeared a few years back. I think Rose would like it but she isn't taking my suggestions these days.

Give me several. When I read, it is like going on holiday. It ain't easy starting motherhood over again at my age, especially when you are seen as an invader. Pippa thinks I'm great so I suppose I should be satisfied. I get lonely though. Rose would not believe it but I too miss her mother. She did wonders with Blair. Now he is hard to reach but healing takes time.

Rose is very like me. At her age, I hid my hurts away from prying eyes and buried myself in books. We'd have so much to share. Let's hope we find each other.

Thanks ahead of time for the books. I'll see you at the bazaar. I'm bringing mustard pickles again.

Yours,
Rosalind

Rose read the signature and stared at the sheet with unbelieving eyes. Grandma needed to get away? From Pippa and herself? Rose knew where her secondhand copy of *Nobody's Girl* had gone. It was in Rose's bedroom on the special shelf. Mum must have borrowed it. She had given it to Rose to read and must have forgotten it really belonged to Grandma. It stood beside the copy of *Ballet Shoes* Mum had found at some book sale.

Rose stood absolutely still, thinking hard. She scarcely noticed Mary's return. She carried several volumes. She smiled at Rose but her face was still flushed.

"Did you get what Grandma wanted?" Rose asked.

"*The Blue Castle* is out. I put in *Daddy-Long-Legs* instead," the librarian said. "And *The Keeper of the Bees*. And, in case she gets fed up with those, I included a new P.D. James mystery that's just been catalogued."

Rose swallowed. Then she pushed Grandma's letter back across the desk to Mary.

"I read it. Thanks for letting me," she said, her own cheeks red.

"I thought it couldn't hurt," her mother's best friend murmured.

"You were right. Come on, Pip," Rose called.

She was quiet on the way home. It must have warmed up. All of a sudden, she could smell spring in the moist wind blowing into her face. She pulled off her mittens, just like her little sister. She stuffed her toque in her pocket too.

When Pippa ran to watch TV, Rose did not follow. Instead she limped out to the kitchen. No Grandma. Rose went upstairs and crept down the hall to Grandma's room. The door stood ajar. She peered in. She did not want to wake Grandma. But Grandma wasn't sleeping; she was reading *Lassie Come Home*.

Her sore foot was propped on a cushion and she did not glance up.

Rose went to her own room. She took down *Nobody's Girl*. Several loose pages fluttered out. She put them back. Grandma would fix it. She was good at fixing broken things.

As Rose started to leave, she glimpsed the spine of *Ballet Shoes*. Slowly she pulled it out and hugged it to her. She had not read it for months. Even if she could no longer dance like Posy Fossil, she could still read about her.

She carried both books to Grandma's room. If her grandmother had not been hard-of-hearing and if she had not been near the end of a great story, she would have heard Rose's dragging step. But she turned a page without looking up.

Rose sat down to wait. There was no rush. What did it matter if supper was late? She and Grandma needed to get away—together. When her grandmother did see her there, Rose would offer to set the table and scramble some eggs. Mum had taught her how to scramble eggs long ago. She and Pippa might even persuade Grandma to eat upstairs. If Dad came home, he could come up too. It would be fun.

Then she opened *Ballet Shoes* and began to read.

Minds

Some minds are like coffins.
Only thoughts that died
Fifty years or so ago
Are shut inside.

Some minds are like pigeonholes
Where thoughts are filed away.
There odds and ends of nothing much
Collect and stay.

Some minds are like highways
Where thoughts keep moving fast,
So intent on gaining time
That life blurs past.

Some minds are like battlefields
Scarred by inner wars.
But April is what happens
In a mind like yours,
For your mind is a garden.
Even under snow,

The seeds of thought within your mind
Take root and grow.
There winter is a seldom
And a short-lived thing
And always there are snowdrops
Hurrying the spring.

At Last

I tried to dissuade that robin
But he simply did not care.
Adamant, he launched snow-ward,
Certain the worms were there.

I told him the wind was bitter.
I warned him it would be grim.
I explained that the fare was meagre
But just try talking to him!

He came . . . and how can I say now,
"You see! I told you so!"
When he saunters, cocky with courage,
His breast a scarlet glow,

And, ignoring his empty stomach
And the ice-enshrouded land,
Carols to all and sundry
Of the family he has planned.